SHOW IT

A Novel

Grace Sidney Harold
Kevin Barry Collopy

Toxurbia Press

To
Chip 'n Dale

"Naked is the best disguise." William Congreve

1. Shakin' It and Makin' It

THE well-built young man steps into the circle of bright white light on the tiny stage in the dark and smoky room, the air thick with the intoxicating mix of feminine fragrances and alcohol. He had never felt comfortable in his skin before he started doing this. Here he was, baring it all three times a night to an audience of female strangers, swaying his hips and gyrating his torso to the beat of ear-piercing prerecorded rhythms. Some of the women whistle, some scream, some throw crumpled-up money at his sneakered feet.

He bends over, squats, and twerks his behind, resulting in a seismic eruption of cheers and catcalls. This guy is god on this stage, alive and free, worshiped by his adoring fans, no longer the shy, awkward boy who stumbled over his words and couldn't look a woman in the eye. Six months into this enigmatic journey, he is the most sought-after performer at The Velvet Joystick strip club. Money, once his primary goal, has become only one facet of his motivation. The thrill of captivating the audience, the licking of lips, the lustful gazes, and the echoing screams, make for a heady cocktail of emotions that have become an intoxicating addiction.

The surge of power wells up inside him as he feels a bold hand slip into the waistband of his jock, while another slides a bill between his smooth, peachy buttocks. "At least they haven't started swiping credit cards back there yet," he mutters under his breath while still maintaining the sensual tempo.

The adrenaline coursing through his body has him stiff as a broomstick within the confines of his blue satin thong. He teeters on the edge of climax as he kicks off an unlaced Nike, nagged by the possibility a frenzied admirer might make off with the prize. To appease the ravenous wolves, he hurls a damp sweat sock into the crowd. "Those damn sneakers cost me a month in tips," he shouts.

As the music fades and the spotlight dims, he jumps down from the stage and retreats to the dingy dressing room at the back of the club. He grabs a towel to dry his short-cropped blonde hair and mop the sweat from his handsome, clean-cut face and toned, athletic body, taking deep gulps of air as he tries to regain his composure. He knows what he needs - a stiff drink, so he pulls on a pair of fight shorts over his thong and pads to the bar.

The club's sultry plush red velvet atmosphere of decadence and desire is in stark contrast with his mundane everyday life. He takes a seat at the bar, his body still trembling with the aftermath of his performance. The barkeep, a burly man with a graying beard named Jimmy, gives him a nod of approval. "You did well up there, Jake. What can I get you?"

He orders a whiskey neat. "And put it on my tab," he says.

Jimmy laughs as he pours a generous shot of whiskey into a glass and slides it in front of Jake. "You mean to tell me there's no room for a wallet in that satin fig leaf?"

The amber liquid shimmers in the dim light and is reflected in his pale blue eyes. Jake takes the glass and holds it up to study it before chugging it in one gulp. The fiery burn hits his throat, and for a moment it is the only thing that matters. The sensation is a welcome distraction from the thoughts and feelings swirling in his head. The whiskey leaves a warm trail inside his chest as it settles in his stomach. He puts the empty glass back on the bar, and Jimmy spies the slight tremor in Jake's hand.

Jake slaps the bar hard. "Hit me again, Jimmy."

"You sure?"

"Fuck, yes, I'm sure," he growls. "Hit me."

The morning lurks only a few hours away, and Jake's thoughts turn to the cold realities of his college classes, his student loan, and the debts that still loom over him. Although he has managed to put a few bucks away over the past few months, it's a drop in the proverbial bucket

2

compared to what he owes. With a sense of resignation that it will be quite some time before he can afford to stop grinding his behind, he looks into the empty glass in front of him and realizes whiskey has become his most trusted companion.

"Take it easy," Jimmy warns as he pours another whiskey neat into the shot glass. "You have two more sets to get through tonight."

"Thanks for the heads-up, *Dad*." Jake tosses his head back, empties the glass, and shivers. "Okay, one more and I'm done."

Jimmy looks at him with sullen eyes. "I'm going to have to cut you off, Jake."

"Just one more, I promise." Jake folds his hands in prayer. "I'm only gonna sweat it out."

"It'll be on my head," Jimmy says. "Tony'll give me my walking papers if he finds out I let one of his boys dance drunk."

"Hey, man, I'm nowhere near drunk." Jake leans across the bar and whispers, "I wanna toast my good buddy Ben."

Jimmy glances at the row of vacant stools lining the bar. "What're you talkin' about?"

"I wanna propose a toast to my good buddy Ben, I said," Jake insists. "In absentia."

"In *absentia*?"

"It means '*not here at the moment*.'"

"I know what it means, college boy." Jimmy shrugs and fills the glass. "So who is this guy Ben?"

"Ben Mendelsen, that's who." Jake lifts his glass in tribute. "I'm livin' the dream 'cause of you, Ben, baby! You beautiful son of a bitch!"

2. The Proposition

THE fluorescent lights in the university library buzzed above Jake's head as he stared at his laptop screen. It was during a late autumn evening six months ago, and he was deep in thought, trying to figure out how to make ends meet. He glanced around at his fellow students, all engrossed in their own struggles, oblivious to his financial concerns. College had turned out to be far more expensive than he had anticipated, and his job as a part-time barista wasn't cutting it. Student loans loomed like a dark cloud on the horizon, threatening to cast a shadow over his dreams of a degree in finance.

Jake took a sip of lukewarm coffee from a disposable cup and sighed, his light blue eyes scanning his financial spreadsheet. Tuition, textbooks, rent, and daily expenses – it was all piling up faster than the money was coming in. He needed a solution, and he needed it fast. He had always prided himself on being resourceful, a quality he had developed growing up in a small, modest household. But this time, he was at a loss.

As he rubbed his temples, trying to massage away his growing headache, his roommate, Ben Mendelsen, came striding into the library, a mischievous grin on his face. Ben was the polar opposite of Jake – outgoing, charming, and always on the lookout for an adventure – and easy sex.

"Hey, Jake." Ben shouted at the top of his voice.

"Shhh!" Jake scanned the annoyed and disturbed faces around them. "Keep it down to a dull roar, okay?"

Ben slid into the chair across the table from Jake. "You look like you've got the weight of the world on your shoulders, bro. What's up? Or should I ask, 'What's *down?*'"

Jake took a moment to formulate his response. He didn't want to whine about his financial woes, but he knew his roommate had a knack for uncovering opportunities. "Only the usual," Jake said with a forced smile. "Bills, tuition, and all that. I need to find a way to make some extra cash."

Ben's grin widened, and he leaned in closer, his voice dropping to a whisper. "Funny you should mention that. I heard about an opportunity that might be right up your alley."

Jake raised an eyebrow, his curiosity piqued. "What kind of opportunity are we talking about here?" He cleared his throat. "Knowing you, I have to ask upfront, is it legal?"

Ben looked around the room before he folded his arms and shot Jake a sly look. "How do you feel about taking your clothes off and shaking your buns for a room full of sex-starved women?"

Jake blinked, caught off guard by the unexpected proposition. "Excuse me?"

Ben laughed a hearty and infectious chuckle. "I'm serious, man. There's a bar downtown that's looking for male strippers. They pay pretty well, too, and you've got the looks for it. Okay, so it's a bit unconventional, but it's an option to consider. When you're thirsty, dirty water can be mighty tasty, right?"

Jake couldn't believe what he was hearing. The idea of becoming a male stripper was something that had never, ever crossed his conservative mind. It sounded absurd, risky, and completely out of character for him. He glanced at his dwindling bank account balance on his laptop screen and had to admit to himself that he was running out of options.

The library, with its hushed atmosphere and the endless cycle of studying, seemed like an entirely different world. Jake's thoughts were in disarray, and he found himself wondering if this unexpected proposition might be the lifeline he desperately needed. He looked at Ben's expectant face and thought, "Could this really be my way out? What's the worst that could happen?"

"Well?" Ben asked with anticipation. "What do you think?"

"Tell me more," Jake said. "And how exactly did this even become a thing with you?"

"This dude in my psych class told me about it," Ben said. "I thought maybe I'd give it a try myself because it sounded hot. All those women watching me. But, shit, I'm in over my head this semester."

Jake looked at him and rolled his eyes. "Plus you don't need the cash 'cause *daddy* is footing the bill for your entire life."

"Well, yeah," Ben said. "There's that."

"So, continue please, genius."

Ben's eyes lit up with excitement. "All right, so here's the deal. The place is called The Velvet Joystick."

"Seriously?"

"Smack on the corner of *Johnso*n and *High* Streets, I kid you not, bro."

"Now, that's pretty funny."

"I know, right? But it's a classy joint. Well, classy enough for a place where dudes jump around naked."

"Wait, wait, wait." Jake took a breath and winced. "Exactly *how* naked are we talkin'?"

"Hey, I've never been there, man," Ben told him, "and the guy didn't really say, but I don't think it's legal in this state for a dude to take out the woolly mammoth in public."

Jake cleared his throat. "Geez, okay, nice to know."

"So you show your ass, man. Big fuckin' deal. Everybody's got an ass."

Jake waved his hands to coax Ben along. "So continue."

"They host ladies only every night after eleven until one, so at least no worries about some creeper dude reaching for your junk."

"One a.m.? Shit, that's kinda late for me."

"No pain, no gain," Ben said. "But they are looking for dudes like you, man – boy-next-door types who are in shape, and are willing to strip down to their skivvies and dance for a crowd of women who've paid a hefty entrance fee for the experience."

Jake couldn't help but feel a mix of apprehension and curiosity. The idea was far from his comfort zone, and he was trying to wrap his head around the concept, but the prospect was tempting, especially given his dire financial situation. "How's the money?"

"They pay dancers a base rate, and the tips are pooled with the other performers, but those tips can mount up fast. Hell, with the other guys there, too, you'll have some camaraderie and probably share a few laughs. It beats the hell out of serving some entitled, over-paid yuppie his half-assed mocha latte half-caff."

Jake leaned back in his chair. The stress of his mounting bills pressed down on him. He met Ben's gaze and took a deep breath. "Kick the tires for me. What are the downsides here?"

Ben hesitated for a moment and scratched his head. He chose his words carefully. "Well, it's not a long-term solution, obviously. It's just a way to make quick money. And there's no room for shyness or stage fright up there, so once your ass is in the spotlight..."

"I guess I need to think about it," Jake said. "It's not something I can decide on the spot."

"Of course, of course." Ben offered a supportive nod. "But keep in mind there are plenty of guys in your financial situation looking for easy work, and an opening that was there yesterday might not be there today."

"I hear you," Jake said.

"Hey, if you think it's for you, maybe, if you want, we can check out the place together." Ben's phone dinged an alert and he jumped up. "Shit, I'm late. See you back in the room. That is, if I don't get lucky."

Jake watched Ben shuffle out the door with phone in hand, and then he returned to his pathetic spreadsheets, but he couldn't shake - *ha* - the image of himself on stage in the nude, okay, so *almost* nude, whatever.

He closed his laptop, shoved it back in its case, and deposited the empty coffee cup in the trash. As he walked towards the exit, he passed a table displaying the new fiction releases recommended by the library staff. One book cover jumped out at him, the title in bold red letters on a stark white background: *GO FOR IT!*

Jake stared at the words in disbelief. "It's an omen," he muttered to himself. "A sign from the gods."

His pace quickened as he left the library, and he found himself yelling at the top of his voice. "Fuck, yes. I'm doing this."

3. The Velvet Joystick

JAKE pushed against the weighty, creaking wooden door, revealing the dusky interior of The Velvet Joystick strip club. The early morning light barely filtered through the windows, casting a melancholy pallor over the place, a testament to a wild night that had unraveled only hours before. His eyes swept the room, taking in the plush red velvet curtains, the bar stocked to the hilt, tabletops adorned with overturned chairs, and the postage-stamp-sized stage divided by a steel pole where he would be expected to shake his stuff.

From behind the bar, Tony, the formidable manager of the establishment, emerged with a presence that demanded attention. In his late forties, Tony's bulky frame, bald pate, and well-manicured goatee gave him an aura of authority. His eyes, sharp and calculating, locked onto Jake as he extended a firm hand.

"Are you Jake?" Tony's question was accompanied by a grip that meant business. He assessed Jake from tousled head to grubby sneakers and then gestured toward a nearby booth.

"This place has character," Jake remarked, attempting to curry favor.

Tony, however, wasn't one for pleasantries. He stared deep into Jake's eyes for a discomfiting moment. "So, you got potential, kid?"

"Thanks," Jake replied, unsure of Tony's intent.

"That was a question, not a compliment," Tony emphasized.

"Oh, sorry."

"I was askin' if you got potential, okay?" Tony punctuated his point by tapping his oversized pinky ring on the table and nodding toward the stage. "Can you picture yourself up there, kid? Heh? Workin' your magic?"

Jake turned to survey the stage. "I think so," he said, nodding.

"So, you got a nice keister?" Tony inquired.

"Excuse me?" Jake was taken aback.

"Again, I'm askin', not complimentin'," he clarified. "Your buttocks, buns, tushy, hiney, ass, whatever? Show it to me, kid."

Jake, feeling trapped and uncomfortable, stood up and turned around. "Like this, you mean?"

"What am I, Superman with X-ray eyes?" Tony retorted. "*Show* it to me! Drop 'em."

"Seriously?"

"Yeah, seriously," Tony affirmed. "Look, I'm not light in my loafers, okay? I'm whatcha call a flesh peddler. I need to inspect the fruits before I sell 'em, ya dig?"

Jake chose not to dissect Tony's peculiar metaphor and decided to comply, undoing his belt and revealing a glimpse of his bare rear end. "Is this okay?"

"Yeah, okay, pull 'em back up." Tony rose and moved back behind the bar, leaving Jake feeling exposed and certain he would never let Ben Mendelsen live this down.

Returning with a Manila folder, Tony placed what looked like a job application on the table in front of Jake. "This job comes with responsibilities and rules," he stated. "You need to read this here paper real careful. These are the dos and don'ts of strippin' at The Velvet Joystick. Follow 'em to the letter. Break 'em, and you're out. No second chances. Got that?"

Jake glanced at the document. "So, this is the application, then?"

"No, sweetheart," Tony corrected him. "This here's your *contract*."

"Really?" Jake was taken aback. "You mean I'm hired?"

"Yeah, how 'bout that? Merry Christmas." Tony tapped the document and continued. "Read it and understand what happens within these here walls *stays* within these here walls. Just like Vegas."

Tony walked back to the bar while Jake skimmed through the document. It outlined expectations, from punctuality and stage presence to maintaining professionalism both inside and outside the club. It also strictly forbade drug use and physical contact beyond what was permitted during performances. Jake thought the rules were pretty straightforward. "So, should I sign it?"

"Do you accept the terms?" Tony said from behind the bar, drying a glass with a towel. "Then sign it. And remember, when you're on that stage, you are the persona you have created, not the guy drowning in student loans."

Jake was taken aback by Tony's omniscient knowledge. "How did you know about my student loans?"

Tony returned, loomed over Jake, and paused for effect before responding. Still holding the glass, he leaned in with a wry smile. "Do I look like I just stepped off the bus from Stupidsville?"

4. Pissin' with the Big Boys

A DAY or so later, Jake found himself anxiously navigating the bustling streets of the city, headed towards The Velvet Joystick for his orientation. As he approached the club's entrance, he couldn't shake the feeling that, no matter what path you choose in life, everything somehow circles back to a classroom situation, complete with its own set of lessons, rules, and expectations.

Stepping through the club's dim and foreboding entrance, Tony greeted him with a nod and led him further inside, guiding him to a private area tucked away behind mirrors and velvet curtains.

Tony, with a demeanor stern and dour, outlined the audition process for new routines and the exacting standards for stage attire. He emphasized the paramount importance of maintaining peak physical condition and provided detailed insights into the club's demanding schedule.

"This job can be a slippery slope," Tony cautioned, his voice carrying a tone of wisdom that had matured since their initial meeting. "It's easy to get caught up in the attention, the money, and the lifestyle. Keep your feet on the ground. Remember, it's a means to an end, not the end itself."

As Tony continued to speak, Jake couldn't help but wonder why the manager sounded a heck of a lot smarter today than he did at their first meeting. The more he listened to Tony, the more he understood that stripping was more than mere dancing; it was an art form, a way of becoming a living fantasy for the club's patrons.

The idea of crafting his own stage persona, of becoming someone entirely different when the spotlight shone on him, excited Jake, and he was eager to embrace the opportunity. He looked forward to refining his routine, meticulously choreographing his movements, and selecting the perfect music to accompany his performance.

Fitness was paramount in this profession, and Jake was determined to maintain a body that would win over the crowd. Tony explained how the other performers were equally committed to honing their physiques, so he wouldn't be alone in this pursuit.

The Velvet Joystick's rigorous schedule now became the central axis around which Jake's life revolved. He had given his notice at the coffee shop and worked out a detailed spreadsheet to balance classes, studying, and work.

Tony introduced Jake to the other "artists" at the club. Marco, the seasoned dancer, had a penchant for classic rock and a devil-may-care attitude. Brett's infectious energy pumped up the entire group, driven by his fervor for fitness. Leo, the self-proclaimed intellectual, brought complexity to his routines, incorporating intricate choreography. And then there was Ethan, whose youthful sensuality and allure had led him to the club only a few days before Jake. There was something undeniably magnetic about Ethan, and Jake found himself drawn to his charm and charisma. These guys were more than mere strippers; each held their unique dreams of success in the world beyond the club's stage.

After their first group meeting, Ethan approached Jake with a warm smile. His dark eyes sparkled with a sensual mischievous gleam. "So, Jake, you and I are the newbies. It might be a good idea for us to stick together," he said in a low, intimate voice.

"Fine with me," Jake said, his nerves calming in Ethan's presence. "I need all the help I can get."

"The other guys seem a bit cliquey," Ethan observed. "And I get that. They've been here a while. But I've been dancing since I was a kid, and I've had more professional training than any of them. I can help you build a routine."

"Sounds great," Jake said, feeling a surge of gratitude for the support.

"That is if you want me to," Ethan said. "I don't want to come off as pushy or anything."

"No, no," Jake reassured him. "Like I said, I'm grateful for the guidance. I have never performed in public before. Not ever. Not even with clothes on."

Ethan's smile deepened as he reassured Jake. "I have a feeling you're a natural, Jake. With your clean-cut college dude looks, they'll be eating right out of your hand."

Jake blushed. "Stop, man. I'm not used to such flattery."

Ethan couldn't resist a mischievous grin. "In fact, I'm sure you could get anyone to eat out of just about anywhere you chose."

5. The Lesson

"I WANT my stage attire to be its own work of art," Ethan Lopez declared, his eyes ablaze with determination as he held court with the other dancers on the edge of the stage at The Velvet Joystick. "You know, something that reflects the character I've adopted."

Marco glanced at the others, a hint of irritation in his eyes, and his voice dripping with sarcasm. "What stage attire? All I do is stuff my sausage and two eggs-over-easy into a *he*-string and go out there and shake it for fifteen minutes."

Ethan, taken aback, struggled to understand. "But Tony told us..."

"Don't take everything Tony says to heart," Marco interrupted with a dose of reality. "He has delusions of grandeur like we're the Chippendale's."

Brett chimed in. "The ladies come to see us take *off* our stage attire. This ain't no fashion show, dude."

"Hey, where's the new boy?" Leo asked.

"Who?" Brett inquired, raising an eyebrow. "You mean Joe College?"

"I'm a new boy, too, you know." Ethan couldn't help but feel like the odd man out.

Marco didn't hold back. "But all that *professional* training makes it seem like you've been around here forever. And ever. And..."

"Actually, Jake is meeting me here in a few minutes," Ethan boasted.

Brett's curiosity piqued. "A date?"

"He asked me to help him put together a routine," Ethan told him.

Marco seized the opportunity to tease. "You can't let all that *professional* training just die on the vine now, can you?"

As the front door of the club swung open, bathing the room in blinding light, Jake bounced in with infectious energy. "What's up, guys?"

"You're in a cheery mood, College," Brett noted.

Jake, stretching and cracking his back, explained. "I'm here to sharpen my stripper moves."

Brett chuckled. "A few late nights sweating under these lights will knock that cheery mood outta you real fast."

"You're in good hands, boy," Leo joked, wiggling his fingers.

"Yeah, very *professional* hands," Marco added, rising majestically to his feet. "Have fun, boys. And no slow dancing, you hear?"

"How 'bout we go to lunch, guys?" Brett proposed. "Let Fred and Ginger glide across the dance floor in private."

"Sounds great," Marco agreed, "I've been here since seven."

"Wish I could join you," Leo sighed. "Alas! The day job awaits!"

"Hey, College, if you're going to dance alone with Ethan, better wear a *cup*." Brett warned, eliciting gales of laughter from Marco and Leo.

Ethan waved them away. "Don't listen to those bitches, Jake. They're just jealous."

As they headed for the door, Marco quipped, "See y'all tonight. And don't forget your stage attire," eliciting more laughter from Leo and Brett as the three amigos exited onto the street.

"What was that about?" Jake asked. "What's this about stage attire?"

Ethan, overwhelmed by the topic, sighed, "Something I said that I shouldn't have said."

Jake was ready for action. "Are we ready to shake our stuff?"

"How long you got?"

Jake checked his phone. "I have class at two, so I'm all yours for an hour and a half."

"Sweet! That'll give us enough time to try out a few dance moves," Ethan told him. "We'll focus on stripping next time. We don't have the right clothes today, anyway." He walked to the control panel and turned on a sexy R&B track to set the mood. He gestured for Jake to join him on the stage.

Jake was surprised to find the stage no wider than a small platform with a silver pole running floor to ceiling. "I thought it would be bigger."

Ethan, not missing a beat, teased, "That's what *she* said."

Jake chuckled, "That line works with anything, doesn't it?"

"Yes, it does." Ethan clapped his hands and assumed a no-nonsense tone. "Okay! Stripping is about more than just taking off your clothes. The dance is the most important part. Without it, you might as well be watching a guy undressing in a locker room. But you have to control the pace, and never look like you're concentrating on yourself." Ethan demonstrated slow, sultry moves with grace and confidence, always keeping his eyes locked on Jake. He moved like a panther, smooth and seductive.

Curious, Jake asked, "Where have you danced before?"

"Tons of places."

"You're so young."

"I'm twenty-six, and I started stripping at sixteen. I lied about my age back then, of course."

"So you don't stay long at each club?" Jake asked.

Ethan shrugged, "Nah, I get itchy feet and need to move on."

Jake nodded and shrugged. "I get that. I guess"

Ethan's expertise captivated Jake, and the lesson went beyond mere technique. It was about embracing the power of their own bodies and connecting with the audience on a deeper level.

"And remember, it's not just about the final reveal," Ethan advised. "It's about the journey, the tantalizing path you lead your audience down. Make them beg for more, and then give them what they want."

"What about the pole?" Jake asked.

"The pole is your friend. Be inventive. You don't need to climb it and twirl on it like some of these showoffs do. Lean up against it, hug it, slide your butt up and down it...Be sexy. You'll figure it out." Ethan clapped his hands. "You're up!"

Jake imitated what Ethan had demonstrated, a bit tentative and awkward at first, but it slowly came together. With each sway of his hips, he felt more connected. "How am I doing?"

"Hold that right there." Ethan, eager to add another layer to the lesson, joined Jake on stage and grabbed his waist to guide his movements to the rhythm. He whispered in his ear, "Feel the music, let it move you."

Ethan was shorter than Jake, but more muscular, and with a head of curly black hair that fell dramatically over his forehead. He moved with grace and elegance, each step measured and smooth. The two of them made a striking stage picture.

"This is incredible." Jake closed his eyes and let himself go, feeling the beat and letting it guide his body.

Ethan pulled Jake's shirt off, revealing a toned and well-defined chest. "Mmm, very, very nice." Then he pulled his own shirt off, exposing his ripped and tattooed torso.

"You're amazing," Jake said.

"Okay, I'm about to get a bit personal now, so don't let it bother you." Ethan's hands ran down Jake's bare back and cupped his butt. "Concentrate on tensing these muscles right here."

Jake surrendered to the moment and the world outside ceased to exist. He felt desired, beautiful, and powerful. As the song came to an end, they stopped and looked at each other, both breathless and exhilarated.

Still catching his breath, Jake said, "That was intense. You've got the moves, man, that's for sure."

Ethan wiped the sweat from his forehead and flashed a mischievous grin. "Damn, dude, I think I *came*."

6. Showtime

THE day of Jake's debut at The Velvet Joystick was, well, one of *those* days. From burning his last piece of toast to spilling coffee on his keyboard, nothing had gone right since he woke up and slapped his bare size ten feet down on his dorm room floor. Even that had been a fiasco because the floor was ice-cold.

"Shit, isn't there any heat in here today?" Jake looked over at Ben, who was cocooned in dreamland, his comforter pulled up tight under his chin.

Jake had planned out his day precisely down to the minute so he would arrive at the club at ten p.m. on the dot and get his nerves under control for when he was scheduled to open the show an hour later. He made it by the hair on his whatever.

"Why am I on first?" Jake asked the guys backstage. "I thought I might get a chance to see you boys in action before I went on."

"Tony is using you as the sacrificial lamb," Leo said. He was standing stark naked, examining himself in the full-length mirror.

"You're fresh meat to reel in the hungry crowd," Marco said.

"Don't worry, Jake," Ethan said. "Just be yourself and you'll be great."

"Easier said than done," Jake sighed.

"Listen to Pollyanna," Brett said. "*She's* had a lot of *professional* training."

"Just be myself?" Jake rolled his eyes. "I thought we were supposed to pretend to be somebody else."

"I told you not to pay attention to the man behind the curtain." Marco scanned Jake's body from head to toe. "So what are you wearing out there?"

Jake looked down at his red Adidas, black sweatpants, and bright yellow Ramones slim-fit t-shirt. "Is this okay?"

A blue satin thong flew from out of nowhere and hit Jake in the face. "With my compliments," Leo said.

"I hope that's been laundered," Brett said.

"I'm wearing new Tommy boxer briefs," Jake said. "Isn't that good enough? It's not what we *wear*, it's what we *don't* wear, right?"

"It's all about the bare ass, baby," Marco told him. "That is the *pièce de résistance*. What did you plan to do, just yank 'em down and moon the ladies?"

"I can't believe I am going to do this," Jake said, plopping down on a wooden chair. "I am so nervous."

"What's to be nervous about?" Marco asked. "Is it the dancing? The audience of hungry women?"

"Maybe his butt crack runs side to side instead of up and down," cracked Leo.

"Thanks, guys," Jake groaned. "You're a big help."

"Better get undressed, Jake, so you can put on the banana hammock and then get dressed *again*," Ethan joked.

Jake undressed in a flash and scrambled into the thong.

Leo clowned around and put his own thong on backward. "This is how you wear it, kid."

"It's his first time," Brett said. "He might think you're serious."

Jake took deep breaths to relax. He put his clothes back on and gave himself the once over in the mirror. "If I were a better Catholic, I'd be praying right now."

Tony swept into the room and growled, "Not a bad idea. God listens to all of us."

"The wizard hears everything," Marco remarked.

Tony clapped his hands. "Okay, listen up." He gave the guys a quick pep talk, then told Jake he was on as the music began to play.

Jake swallowed hard. "Now?"

"Yeah, now!" Tony replied. "Get your ass out there!"

Jake took a deep breath, closed his eyes, and whispered a small prayer. He could feel his heart pounding against his chest, and his palms were sweaty. He knew this was the moment he had been waiting for, and it would change his life forever.

When he stepped onto the stage, the roar of the crowd was deafening. The stage lights were so bright he couldn't make out any faces. All he could see was a heavy fog in front of him. The loud music pulsated, the bass vibrated through his feet, and he felt like he was in a dream. As his eyes adjusted to the glare, a sea of women of all ages, shapes, and sizes, came into focus, their lustful eyes on him alone.

He began to dance, haltingly at first, swaying his body in awkward jerks to the rhythm of the music and gyrating to the beat, but a bit off balance and a tad out of step. Determined to keep their attention, he lifted his shirt, revealing his toned abs, and the crowd howled with delight. He could feel his confidence growing with each passing moment and moved closer to the edge of the stage. An older woman reached out to touch him, and the electricity of allowing a stranger that privilege sent shivers down his spine. He spun around, tucked his thumbs into the waistband of his sweatpants, and, after hesitating a moment, lowered them just a smidge to tease. He spotted the other dancers watching from the shadows and saw Ethan raising his arms high above his head to give him two thumbs up.

Jake became lost in the moment, swooning to the music and overcome by the passion of the crowd. When he jerked his pants to the floor, and his toned backside was finally revealed in all its masculine glory, the audience erupted into cheers. He was relieved it was out there with nothing more to fear. The thong felt foreign against his skin, but he pushed through the discomfort, letting his body take over and move with wild abandon, a blur of motion and energy. The music reached its climax, the screams were at a fever pitch, women pelted him with money, and Jake knew he was in total control. Grabbing the pole, he bent over and invited a few women to cop a feel.

As the music faded, Jake knew his time on stage was coming to an end, so he struck a final dramatic pose that left the audience gasping for breath. He had danced his heart out, giving them everything he possibly could.

Walking offstage to the cheers of the crowd, the letdown felt like when he was a kid and the roller coaster brought him back to the station after a heart-stopping ride. The experience took more out of him than he would have imagined, and he leaned against the wall panting and sweating and attempting to catch his breath. He couldn't get his mind around what he had just done, but he knew he was hooked.

A round of applause and whoops of joy greeted him in the dressing room as the other guys slapped him on the back with shouts of "Way to go!" and "You did it, man!"

Tony popped in wearing a wide smile. "A few rough spots, kid, but not a bad first outing."

Jake Whitney had earned his stripes and had proven himself one of the team. He was a stripper now, and there was no turning back.

7. Afterglow

THE morning sun streamed through the small dorm room window and cast a warm glow upon the disordered scene within—textbooks scattered across the floor, a mound of laundry spilling from the hamper, and two bodies stirring from their restless slumber. Ben let out a mighty yawn and stretched, his body playing a symphony of pops and cracks. He glanced at the clock. It was five to seven.

"Hey, Jake, you awake?"

Jake grumbled. "No."

Ben stifled another yawn. "What the hell time did you crawl in?"

Jake croaked, "Fuck, I dunno." He made a weak attempt at stretching.

Ben pushed himself upright and rubbed the sleep from his eyes. "It was after two, I know that."

Jake pulled the covers up and over his head to resist the intruding morning. "Well, yeah," he admitted with a sigh. "The show was over at one, so...yeah."

"How 'bout we grab some breakfast and you can tell me all about it?" Ben suggested as he shuffled towards the bathroom. "But right now I gotta pee like Secretariat." With the bathroom door closed behind him, he shouted, "I got the first shower."

Jake's head popped out from under the covers to yell, "And no *pissing* in the shower."

Emerging into the crisp embrace of autumn air, the two guys trudged across the campus, the fallen leaves crunching beneath their worn-out sneakers on the way to the college cafeteria.

The place hummed like a beehive as Jake slumped into a chair at a secluded corner table. "I just want coffee."

"I could eat a dead rhinoceros," Ben announced. "You better start eating right, too, and thinking healthy, bro, or these twenty-hour days are gonna kill you."

"Nineteen," Jake corrected, squinting at his friend through half-closed bloodshot eyes.

"Huh?" Ben leaned in, concerned.

"Yesterday was a *nineteen*-hour day," Jake clarified, resting his head on his hand. The heavy toll of his late-night endeavor was apparent.

"Sit tight," Ben told him. "I'll get you coffee. Try to stay awake, okay?"

As Jake watched Ben take his place in the chow line, he knew deep in his heart that his friend was right. If only one night had kicked his ass this hard, he wondered how he would cope with the grueling schedule of performing night after night, possibly as much as six times a week, that is, if he aimed to maximize his earnings.

"Oh, but what a night it was," Jake whispered to himself. The memories of his first dance performance at The Velvet Joystick filled him with a sense of euphoria. The music, the lights, the enthusiastic audience, the women who watched him with fascination, the adrenaline, and the fear—all of it combined to bring a smile to his face.

"Hey, Jakee-Jakee, time to wakee-wakee." Ben's voice snapped Jake back to reality. He blinked and found his friend holding a steaming cup of coffee. Had he dozed off?

"Drink up," Ben urged, handing the cup to Jake. "I'll get you another one in a bit. You should ditch all your classes today, bro, and spend the rest of the day in bed. Take a mental health day."

"I can't," Jake replied, sipping the coffee with caution. "I'm swamped." He grimaced as the scalding liquid burned his tongue. "Jesus, what do they do, boil this stuff?"

Ben settled down at the table with a tray of eggs, sausage, potatoes, and toast. "So, how'd it go last night?"

Jake glanced around to ensure no one was within earshot, before leaning in closer to Ben. "It was insane, man. The place was packed, and they fuckin' *loved* me."

"Did anybody grab your junk?" Ben asked between bites.

"Uh, yeah," Jake boasted.

"No way," Ben said, chewing. "Was she hot?"

"Not bad," Jake replied with a sly grin, "if you like 'em around *sixty*."

Ben's face contorted in disgust. "And you let her?"

"Well, you wouldn't want to be rude to the paying customers," Jake said with a nonchalant shrug. "She stuffed a fiver down there. Deep, too."

"Five bucks to touch a twenty-one-year-old pecker?" Ben pumped his fist. "*Ka-ching.* The bitch got away with murder."

Jake defended himself. "Those fivers add up, too. By the way, dinner is on me tonight."

"Why?"

"It's payback for setting me on the road to sin and degradation," Jake quipped.

"Well, thank *yuh*, thank *yuh,* very much," Ben said, channeling his inner Elvis. "I owed you one for my knee, so now we're even."

Jake screwed up his face. "Your knee?"

"The roller park thing, remember?" Ben pulled up his pant leg to reveal a small scar. "It would look a lot worse if you hadn't practically carried me to the emergency room."

"It would look even *better* if you hadn't tried to be Tony Hawk," Jake said. "And those girls didn't even notice."

"Whatever, dude! Life is an adventure," Ben said. "Speaking of adventures, when can I come see you shake yer boo-tay?"

"Never."

"Why not?"

"Dude, I would die of embarrassment."

"You forget," Ben told him. "We're roomies and I've seen your sorry ass. Seriously, it does nothing for me."

"It has nothing to do with my *ass*," Jake retorted. "It's all the other stuff I have to do. I could only move around like that knowing *nobody* out there has the slightest idea who I am."

"So, I *can't* come see you?" Ben asked wide-eyed. "For real?"

"Sorry." Jake stuck out his bottom lip in mock sympathy. "Ladies only."

"Shit." Ben's eyes sparked with mischief. "So I'll come in drag."

Jake, still weary, shook his head. "Way too scary to even think about on an empty stomach." He folded his arms on the table and rested his head.

"Alright," Ben sighed. "But when you're rich and famous, I'm coming after you for some glitzy show biz special privileges."

Jake couldn't help but smile. "I'll give you a special privilege. You can polish my solid gold g-string collection."

Ben licked his lips. "I'll give every one of 'em the yummy test."

Jake picked up a piece of Ben's toast and tossed it at him. "How old are you? *Nine?*"

8. Letting It All Hang Out

IN THE days following, Jake's newfound passion for stripping was fueled by the enthusiastic applause and support of his audience. His determination to refine his skills led him to immerse himself in the world of dance. He watched countless performance videos on YouTube and even ventured onto some less-than-reputable websites to gain inspiration and knowledge on the art of stripping.

His tireless practice sessions at the school gym became a regular routine. He worked on perfecting his moves, rhythm, and expression, and explored a wide range of dance styles, from contemporary to hip-hop. The result was a unique blend of dance performance both mesmerizing and emotionally resonant, captivating his growing fan base of ecstatic females.

The Velvet Joystick became a second home for Jake, and with each performance, he grew increasingly comfortable on stage. It was during these moments he realized dance was a lot more than simply moving to music; it was a form of communication and a powerful means of expressing emotions and telling a story.

One evening, after yet another exhilarating performance, Jake stepped off the stage to the applause of a cheering crowd. The bright lights dimmed, but the music continued to pulse through the speakers. There would be no encore tonight, though, because he was drained and depleted.

"You were terrific, kid." Tony gushed. "You had 'em on their feet. You should be proud of yourself."

Jake's heart swelled with a mixture of relief and joy. He couldn't pinpoint what had triggered Tony's exuberant response because he had done nothing especially different. He knew something was amiss.

"So, I been thinkin," Tony began.

"About?" Jake continued to towel off, sensing something significant was about to be revealed.

"I think the time has come for you to push the envelope," Tony said. "That is, if you think you're ready."

"Push the envelope?" Jake squinted with puzzlement. "Like how do you mean?"

"I'll foot the bill for some cheap g-strings," Tony explained. "You hear what I'm sayin'?"

Jake shook his head. "Uh, frankly, no, I don't."

"*Disposable* ones," Tony clarified. "Ya dig? You'll toss one out at each show."

Jake's eyes widened in realization. "You mean, I'll be standing up there...?"

Tony nodded with a wicked grin. "Kid, if I had your body, I'd prance around naked all day swingin' that thing for anybody who wanted a look."

Jake was taken aback. "What about the other guys? Will they be...?"

"They don't got what you got, kid," Tony interrupted. "They look too...*available*. You're classy goods." He gestured with a thumb and forefinger, punctuated by an air kiss, as if he had just tasted the world's greatest pasta sauce.

"Thanks for the kind words," Jake said, "but is this even legal?"

"No worries," Tony assured him. "The cops are in our pocket because of what we stuff in theirs."

Jake started to see life at The Velvet Joystick from a different perspective. Was there more to it than meets the eye? He shrugged, "What the hell, it's only a *dick*, right?"

Tony chuckled. "We'll put up a '*Private Party*' sign. I mean, this here is a *party*, right? And we're gonna be showin' 'em some *privates*, ain't we?" Tony enjoyed his own joke so much he choked on it.

"Well, I'll give it the old college try, Tony," Jake agreed, plagued by doubt. "But if I chicken out..."

"You won't chicken out, kid," Tony said with confidence. "Not when you're standin' up to your *goody bag* in cash."

"So when do you want me to do this?" Jake asked.

Tony pondered for a moment, rubbing his chin. "I can have a case of them cheap rocket pockets here by Friday, so you good with Saturday night?"

Jake gave it a moment's consideration, and then nodded with determination. "Saturday it is."

Tony jerked his head back to emphasize the need for confidence. "I don't want you blabbin' to the other boys what your gonna be doin', okay?"

"Sure," Jake nodded. "Okay."

"I want it should be a surprise," Tony stated, "'cause, hand to god, no other dancer has ever hung his meat out on this here stage before."

Jake winced at Tony's vivid choice of words, but he nodded in agreement. "I hear ya."

"And one more thing."

"What one more thing?" Jake asked, dreading the response.

Tony grabbed Jake by the elbow and led him to a corner of the club where the lighting was better. "Lemme see it real quick," he whispered.

"Excuse me?"

"I may have some advice, is all." Tony tapped his pinky ring on Jake's thong. "Show it to me."

"Well, I sup-pose," Jake said, looking around the room, hoping no one was watching. He pulled the thong away from his body.

After a quick glance, Tony shook his head. "I figured as much."

"What's wrong with it?" Jake felt inadequate. He let go of the thong and it snapped back in place.

"Well, see, I had a gardening job when I was a kid," Tony explained. "Part time, you know, in the summer?"

Jake struggled to follow Tony's train of thought. "Okay, but what does that...?"

"I learned that trees look *taller* when there's no *shrubbery* 'round 'em." Tony gave him a wink of encouragement. "Somethin' to consider, if you catch my drift."

9. Mowing the Lawn

JAKE'S morning had begun with a single mission: reclaim his privacy for the delicate and solitary task of manscaping, a ritual best kept far away from the prying eyes of friends, family, neighbors - and roommates.

Ben's voice pulled him from his thoughts. "Why are you draggin' your feet this morning, dude?" Ben scoured the room for his missing sneaker. "You're still in your PJs."

"I've got some stuff I want to finish before I head out," Jake replied with mock casualness.

Ben, dressed and ready for the day, hoisted his backpack over his shoulder. "If you want to grab lunch, meet me in the caf at noon."

"Sounds good," Jake replied, suppressing a sigh of relief as Ben finally left the room. With the coast clear, Jake didn't want to beat around the bush. (Oops!)

He headed straight to the bathroom for a hot shower, hotter than usual to prevent any unwelcome shrinkage. He needed his testicles relaxed and hanging loose so they would be easier to move around while he shaved them.

Emerging from the shower, towel-wrapped and determined, Jake was ready to face the challenge. His research had led him to the conclusion that most shaving-related injuries occurred in the treacherous terrain of the scrotum, a daunting battlefield where a wrong move could invoke the theme from *Jaws*, which is why Jake ruled out the way-too-risky electric razor for that delicate task. Since he was already a seasoned user of a safety razor for his face, he was pleased it was also the Internet pubic hair gurus instrument of choice. But he knew better than to rush into the job singing "*Figaro! Figaro!*" like he was the Barber of Seville, no matter how safe the razor claimed to be.

Over the years, his locker room experience had taught him that guys with darker hair always sported a bushier hedge down there. His pubic forest wasn't too dense at all. He had been blessed with light, blonde follicles that had persisted from his teenage years. So, after carefully trimming the area with scissors, he applied a generous layer of shave cream. He was meticulous, cleaning the blade every few strokes to prevent any hair from jamming it. It didn't take long before the overgrown shrubbery had been cleared from the playground, and he also took care to tidy up a few annoying stray hairs on the shaft. All this pampered attention, however, had given him a chubby, which he promised to address during the rinse-off when he was through gardening.

But now it was time for the delicate part. He balanced on one leg with the other propped up on the toilet, his scrotal skin pulled as taut as possible. Slow, careful strokes with gentle pressure followed, all in the direction of the hair growth. He stretched the skin to prevent nicks, recalling the past discomfort of razor burn on his face and unwilling to repeat the experience on his love pouch. "Why does a guy's junk have to be so wrinkled and saggy?" he mumbled. "God must be an underachiever."

After what felt like an eternity of precision work, there was one more problem area to tackle. Jake searched the vanity and found a small hand mirror, which he positioned on the floor for a better view of the no-man's land between his sack and his crack. "Nice view," he chuckled to himself.

After a second shower, patting himself dry, and taking a few seconds to rub out his pesky arousal as a reward for his labors, Jake admired his handiwork in the mirror and gave himself two thumbs up. *Voilà*. He was quite pleased with his new bare appearance, even if his package looked like he borrowed it from a ten year old.

When he opened the bathroom door, Jake came face-to-face with an unexpected surprise: Ben had returned with an urgent case of the "wee-wee shivers."

"I didn't think you were ever coming out," Ben said, his voice tinged with desperation. "I have to pee like Whirlaway."

Jake froze, hardly believing his roommate's timing. "I thought you left for the day."

"I forgot my psych book," Ben explained. Then his eyes widened as he squeezed by Jake to get to the toilet. "Dude! What the hell happened to your *fluff*?"

10. Very Dirty Dancing

STANDING backstage, waiting for his cue, the minutes ticked by like hours. Jake wasn't sure if he was ready for this. He was dressed in a vibrant new ensemble of sleek black pants and a crimson silk shirt that Tony had surprised him with at the last minute, telling him, "A star needs to dress like a star."

Since the new outfit clashed with his scuffed red Adidas, Tony suggested Jake make his entrance barefoot. He believed it would not only be more provocative but also eliminate the awkward, time-consuming process of shedding shoes and socks during the strip, which always came across as clunky. The smoothness of the fabric in the new black pants allowed them to slide off easier, but the cheap g-strings Tony ordered from a wholesale remainder warehouse were coarse and stiff, and they chafed like crazy. Jake was *almost* looking forward to slipping the nasty thing off to let itchy and scratchy breathe again.

Jake was no fool. He figured he was a pawn in Tony's scheme to take the club's reputation to the next level with more show-stopping action to give the customers what they wanted. And what they *apparently* wanted was a full frontal assault of voyeurism, which was fine with Jake as long as Tony gave him a decent cut of the action to put that irksome student loan firmly in his rearview mirror.

When the music revved up and the lights came on, Jake knew he had no choice but to get out on that stage and give it his all. And tonight he was truly going to give his *all*. He kicked off the flip-flops he had worn backstage to protect his clean feet from the club's grimy floor and sauntered onto the stage. The rhythm of the music vibrated through the wooden floor, and now Jake could feel it in his toes, synchronizing his movements with the intoxicating tempo of the music.

The red shirt reflected the spotlight like a beacon, and he slowly unbuttoned it, slipped it from his shoulders, and tossed it behind him.

39

The screams from the crowd were jubilant as Jake's hand slid down his glistening chest to untie the string holding up his pants, and he could feel heated desire radiating off the crowd in waves as they anticipated his next move. When Jake yanked 'em down and revealed a tight black thong much smaller than usual, a collective gasp released from the audience. Jake tugged on the fabric, pulling it away from his body with one finger as if testing its limits, teasing with a shaded outline of what rested beneath. When he let go and the thong snapped back into place, the audience's unified pang of disappointment reverberated through the room.

Tony watched from the sidelines, tapping his clunky pinky ring against his thigh in rhythm with the music, and keeping a close eye on the other boys. He wanted them to witness Jake's big reveal, his sneaky way of announcing that Jake had become his star attraction. However, their routines had become old hat to each other by then, and they no longer paid much attention when another dancer was on. The one exception was Ethan, who made sure he was there to watch Jake every night with rapt fascination.

Jake took a deep breath and decided it was time to give them what they came for. His fingers tapped a tantalizing path to the waistband of his g-string. As he fidgeted with it, he couldn't help but feel a growing sense of dread. He had been shy all his life, even in a locker room situation with other guys, so what on God's green earth had possessed him to agree to dance in the nude in front of a room full of women? He'd strutted his stuff in little more than a fig leaf for weeks, so why would he suddenly have second thoughts about going the final distance to expose a body part half the population owned, and the other half was more than likely on speaking terms with? *"Fuck it,"* he mumbled to himself, and took a deep breath as he tucked his thumbs into the waistband of his g-string.

Ethan couldn't contain his excitement. "Guys, get over here. I think Jake is going Full Monty."

They gathered around, astonished and concerned, shouting "No way!" and "What the hell!" and "Aren't you going to stop him, Tony?"

So as not to show his hand, Tony hesitated for a moment. "I dunno, let's see what the boy's made of."

Marco gasped, "Holy moly, he's going for it."

"Has he lost his mind?" Brett shouted.

Leo exclaimed, "The dude's got balls."

"And we're about to see *both* of 'em," Ethan sighed.

With every eye in the place fixed on him, the suspense in the room ramped up to an eleven out of ten. Jake's trembling hands inched the g-string down past the point of no return and closer to the moment of total exposure. His heart raced in tandem with the crowd's anticipation, and with one final, audacious tug, he let the little black itchy thing flutter to the stage floor, revealing his smooth, toned, twenty-one-year-old anatomy in all its naked-as-the-day-he-was-born glory.

Leo laughed out loud. "Whoops, there it is."

"Damn!" cried Marco.

Brett was awestruck. "Talk about stepping out of your comfort zone."

"Damn, he even *shaved* it," Ethan murmured, as he gawked in astonishment.

The room shook from an eruption of cheers, whistles, and applause, a symphony of support and excitement for a shy guy who had found his courage in the most unexpected of places. In that revealing moment, Jake found a sense of empowerment, and he continued to dance, more unapologetic and uninhibited than before, unaffected by his total nudity and proud he was giving the audience what they had craved.

The line between performer and exhibitionist blurred as the electrifying connection between Jake and the audience intensified, leaving everyone in the room breathless and wanting more. Everyone except his rivals at the club – Marco, Brett, and Leo – who, at the same moment, came to the realization that their spotlight had dimmed at the ascension of The Velvet Joystick's new "star".

Even Ethan wondered if Jake had become a threat to his future when he noticed Tony beaming like the Cheshire Cat. "Looks like the teacher has a new pet," Ethan muttered.

"Keep givin' and givin', kid," Tony shouted toward Jake. "Make 'em beg for more and more."

But, Jake wondered, how much more, exactly, was a guy expected to give?

11. Balancing Act

MONDAY morning rolled around with its usual feeling of dread for Jake. Calculus class would require all his attention, followed by back-to-back lectures in history and finance. It was his night off from the bar, at least, but it wasn't enough to stem the tide of looming deadlines and assignments. Even shaving had become an added burden, and not only his face. He now had the additional task of taking care of the stubble *down yonder*, as well. God forbid his fans notice a five o'clock shadow around eleven at night.

"So do your balls itch?" Ben asked, biting into a slice of toast during breakfast in the college cafeteria.

"They itched at first," Jake said, getting irritated. "Listen, can we please talk about something other than my balls?"

"Okay, sorry." Ben chomped into a sausage. "Does your dick itch?"

Jake jumped up and grabbed his backpack. "I'm outta here."

Ben reached out to stop him, his tone more sincere now. "I'm only messin' with you, dude. Geez, chill."

Jake slouched back in the chair, his frustration simmering. "I feel like I'm gonna blow a gasket."

"So blow me instead," Ben said with a grin, attempting to lighten the mood.

Jake put his head down on the table. "I don't need your jokes right now."

"I'm trying to cheer you up, that's all."

"I know, I know," Jake sighed, sitting up again and releasing a long breath. "Too much shit, too little time. The pressures keep multiplying, like those brooms in that Mickey Mouse cartoon."

"So quit the day job," Ben advised. "Correction: night job."

"I'd rather quit school," Jake exclaimed. "I need the dough, whether I stay in school or not."

"I feel responsible," Ben said.

43

"You didn't hold a gun to my head and say 'Strip or else.'"

"I thought it would lessen your troubles," Ben said, "not add to them."

"I feel like Stretch Armstrong," Jake said, "and two angry kids are pulling me in two different directions."

"I had one of those," Ben chirped. "Do you have any idea what's inside those things?"

Jake shrugged, not really giving a damn. "Some kind of liquid plastic, I imagine."

"Maple syrup."

"No way."

"Way," Ben nodded with confidence. "Me and Billy Teazle cut one open and it got all over his parents' carpet. Ugly way to die."

"Cut me open while you're at it," Jake sighed, his gaze fixed on the table. "I can't see a way out. I need the money, and I can't afford to screw up my education either."

Ben nodded in understanding. "You need to find a way to make it work, dude, or you're gonna snap."

Jake looked up with desperation in his eyes. "Do you have a magical solution hidden up your sleeve?"

Ben chuckled. "Maybe you can find a way to prioritize what truly matters and cut out the stuff that doesn't. Like, do you really need to *shave*, you know, down *there* every day? That must take a lot of time."

Jake considered this. "Maybe I've been overdoing it, trying too hard to be perfect."

"It's time you gave yourself a break, dude. Grooming your Johnson is not an essential part of life. Seriously, most women expect to find a hedge down there. I haven't had any complaints."

Jake's shoulders tensed. "Yeah, but there's Tony."

Ben slammed his fist down on the table. "Fuck Tony."

Jake jumped, startled, and stammered, "He's...my...*boss*. I can't just..."

A light bulb lit up over Ben's head and he snapped his fingers. "Tell him you're breaking out in a terrible rash. I'm sure he won't want customers to see that."

Jake shrugged and sighed. "That might work, but it's only one of the many fires I need to put out."

Ben threw his hands up in triumph. "Dude, it's a start. Solve one problem at a time."

Jake was dubious. "You make it sound so easy."

Ben leaned forward and conveyed his earnestness with a serious gaze. "Talk to your professors about pushing back deadlines, and tell Tony you need a night off or you won't be able to work at all. They may be more reasonable than you think."

Jake nodded. "I suppose I can give it a try."

Ben gave Jake an encouraging smile. "Hey, if you don't ask, you don't get."

"That psych class is really paying off," Jake said with a chuckle. "You'd make a hell of a shrink."

"That'll be a hundred bucks, sir, for the hour." Ben chuckled.

Jake leaned back in his chair, his mind racing. "I needed this conversation more than you know."

Ben winked. "Anytime, bro. After all, I got you into this fix."

Jake spent the rest of the morning and early afternoon in classes, his mind wrestling with Ben's advice. It was clear he needed a change, but the path forward was still hazy. The mounting deadlines and assignments kept gnawing at him, making it difficult to focus on anything else.

A heavy sigh of relief escaped his lips as he stepped out of the lecture hall for the last time that day. When he checked his phone, a text from Tony stared back at him, demanding he come in and work that night at the bar because Brett and Marco had called off.

Jake's outlook had enjoyed a hopeful afternoon in a ray of sunshine, but now the storm clouds were gathering again.

12. Benny the Dip

BENJAMIN Mendelsen hesitated, chewed his lip, and worked up the courage to press 'Dad' in the list of contacts on his iPhone. He swallowed hard and waited for the call to connect.

"Well, well, well," a familiar voice on the other end greeted him. "Look who is still among the living."

"Hey, Dad," Ben replied, taking a deep breath to steady his nerves. "What's up?"

"*What's up?*" the voice replied. "That's all you have to say after, what has it been, a *month* not hearing from you?"

"Sorry, Dad, I've been super busy."

"I've called, I've texted. There's no excuse." The voice bristled with controlled anger. "I assume you're still in school since they're cashing the tuition checks."

"Yes, I'm still in school."

"Barely passing, I'll bet."

"I'm doing okay," Ben said. "Listen, Dad..."

"*Listen, Dad.*" The voice mimicked and mocked him, dripping with sarcasm. "That only means one thing. You're out of money again."

Ben Mendelsen may have offered advice to others with the same finesse as Lucy van Pelt from the Peanuts comic strip, but as for being his own counsel, well, not so much. Born into a world free from financial concerns, Ben sported a tall, well-proportioned frame that radiated a natural devil-may-care confidence. His chiseled jawline, messy chestnut hair, and piercing green eyes were irresistible confections to women, especially those drawn to expert sex, and garnished with a sprig of fresh danger, all cleverly packaged in designer clothes that advertised his affluent background.

"Well, now that you mention it," Ben winced, immediately realizing it was the wrong way to start.

The voice let out an exasperated gasp. "You aren't taking any of this seriously, are you? Where's the money going, son? What the hell are you doing with it?"

"Stuff's expensive, Dad."

"Don't you mean *girls* are expensive? *Women* are expensive? And I'm not bailing you out the next time you don't wear protection."

"What do you want me to say, Dad?" Ben asked the voice.

"*What do I want you to say?* Jesus Christ. Aren't you old enough to know what to say? We have given you every *fucking* advantage."

Ben tried to keep it together. "I know you have," he said.

"You aren't giving money to that loser roommate of yours, are you?" the voice accused him.

Ben shifted from foot to foot. "I may have helped him out a few times, Dad, but it's not like he's taking advantage of me." *Thank you, Jake Whitney, and a big wet kiss on your hairless balls for being the best fucking excuse a bad boy ever needed.*

The voice became impatient. "You can't keep bailing him out."

"You and mom taught me that charity begins at home, didn't you, Dad?" Ben had to hold the phone away because he couldn't trust himself not to laugh out loud.

"You better not be funding his drug habit or anything," the voice warned.

"Well, he has his share of problems, but he's not a druggie. I mean, I'm his roommate, I'd know."

The line went quiet for a moment. Ben could practically hear the voice's frustration through the phone. Finally, the voice echoed a mix of disappointment and concern. "Ben, you have your whole life ahead of you, and I want the best for you. But you can't keep pouring your money into someone else's troubles. You need to be responsible and focus on your own future."

Ben nodded, even though the voice couldn't see it. "I understand, Dad. I'll be more careful with my spending."

48

The voice's tone softened a bit. "I'll make a deposit in your account in the morning. I just worry about you, that's all. You're a good kid, but you've got to be smarter about your choices."

"I know, Dad," Ben replied, waving his middle finger at the phone and miming a jerk off. "I'll make some changes, I promise." *Please end this call before I piss my pants laughing.*

The voice sighed, and became more compassionate. "That's all your mother and I want, Ben. She worries herself sick about you. Take care of yourself. And please call us more often. The money doesn't mean anything, you know that."

"I'm grateful for the support, Dad. Love to mom." A smile crossed Ben's face as he clicked off the call, content he had reeled in his gullible father one more time. *"The money doesn't mean anything,"* he muttered to himself. "Fuck, he expects me to believe that pile of horseshit? Well, he can kiss my white All-American ass in Macy's window during the Thanksgiving Day parade!"

Ben's pace picked up as he dodged rush-hour traffic and bounced across the car, truck, and bus snarled avenue. As he pushed open the glass door and walked in, his easy smile and charismatic charm masked the anxiety and desperation he felt as he pulled the new hundred-dollar bill out of his wallet and slid it under the Off Track Betting window to place it all on the two-year old favorite, Handy Dandy, to win in the last race of the day at Pimlico.

• • • •

13. Dangerous Curves

WITH the stage bathed in a kaleidoscope of colorful lights, the pulsating bass of the music reverberated through the dance club. Jake's movements were precise. His body flowed with the beat and glistened with sweat. He grabbed the pole, lifted his feet off the stage, and spun around, his muscles flexing with each movement. His eyes scanned the crowd, and that's when he spotted her.

Impeccably dressed and groomed, sipping white wine at a table close to the stage, her elegant presence was a contrast with the club's usual raunchy energy. As Jake danced, his eyes repeatedly found their way back to her. She appeared to be in her late forties, maybe fifty, with perfectly styled dark hair, languid brown eyes, and lips painted a deep shade of red that advertised confidence and sensuality.

When the music stopped and Jake took a bow, the elegant woman crooked her finger for him to come closer. He leaned in, hoping for a tip.

"Care to join me for a drink?" she whispered, her lips close to his ear.

"Sorry, but it's against the rules for dancers to mingle with the guests," he replied.

"I'll take care of that," she assured him. "Go freshen up."

"What the hell?" Jake muttered to himself, feeling intrigued but cautious about her privileged attitude. After waving to the crowd, he headed to the dressing room, eager to finish for the night. It was finally time to get out of there and head home to bed after a long-ass day, and another one tomorrow that was waiting to pop up like Kleenex.

The other dancers had left, and Jake was alone in the dressing room when Tony appeared. "We've received a special request," he said.

"What's that?" Jake inquired.

"One of our best customers asked if you'd join her for a drink."

"Oh, her," Jake recalled. "I told her it was against the rules."

Tony exhaled. "Sometimes rules are meant to be broken, kid."

"You want me to have a drink with her?"

"Hey, the other guys are gone, so nobody'll know. I'll set up a table in my office," Tony reasoned. "What's the harm, right?"

Jake hesitated. "I have early classes in the morning, Tony."

"Fifteen minutes," Tony bargained. "Twenty at most."

"If she's such a good customer," Jake asked, "how come I've never seen her before?"

"She usually sits way in the back," Tony explained. "But she sat up front tonight to get a good look at you." His wink was a plea.

"Fifteen minutes," Jake agreed. "Let me clean up."

A few minutes later, Jake entered Tony's office, which had been transformed into a romantically lit dining area with a linen cloth on the table, a candle, and two glasses of wine. He made his way over to the table, trying to ignore his racing heart, and extended his hand. Her black dress accentuated her figure, and her long blondish hair fell in soft waves around her shoulders. Jake was captivated by her words, her confidence, and her mysterious knowledge of him.

She leaned in close, her voice sultry as she whispered, "You're not like the others, Jake. I can see it in your eyes. You're different, and that's what drew me to you tonight."

"Thank you, Ma'am," he replied. "That's very kind."

"Ma'am? Did you really call me *Ma'am*?" She threw her head back and laughed.

"Did I say something wrong?" Jake looked sheepish.

"It's so *outré*, so hopelessly middle class." Still giggling, she took a sip of wine. "Please call me Veronica. I'm so sorry, I didn't mean to be rude."

"Not at all," he said. "I'm not the world's most sophisticated guy."

"I've traveled the world and I've experienced so much," she told him, her gaze unwavering. "But I've never met someone as intriguing as you, Jake."

Jake found himself entangled in a sea of emotions as he sat across from Veronica. Her words and the way she looked at him were enchanting. He sipped his wine, feeling its warmth spreading through him. "This is quite unexpected," he confessed.

Veronica leaned in closer and whispered, "Life is full of surprises, Jake. Sometimes the most unexpected moments become unforgettable ones."

After a few minutes of pleasantries passed, Jake checked his phone. "Wow! Time is whizzing by tonight."

Veronica shook her head. "Where would you young people be without your silly devices?"

"I hate to cut this short," he said, "but I have early classes tomorrow."

"A college boy? How exciting!" Veronica smiled, her eyes looking both disappointed and sensuous. "I understand, Jake. Duty calls. It's a good thing to be responsible."

Jake flashed Tony thumbs up as he walked out the door, and Tony returned to his office to sit at the table across from Veronica, who was studying herself in a compact mirror with intense concentration.

"So," Tony said. "You like?"

Veronica snapped the compact shut and flashed her lynx eyes. "Yes, I very much *like*," she purred.

14. Limited Offer

THE neon sign buzzed outside the nondescript bar, casting a flickering, crimson glow on the rain-slicked pavement. Inside, the air hung heavy with the scent of alcohol and the hum of conversation. Jake sat at the bar nursing one of his nightly bourbons during the lull between shows, when Tony passed by and leaned in. "I've got somethin' for you, kid," he rasped, his voice a low growl beneath the deafening din. "It's an opportunity for you to make some nice money." He gestured toward his office.

Jake glanced up from the worn wooden bar, his brow furrowed with curiosity. He wondered: *Had another rich bitch requested some private time?* He threw back the bourbon in one swallow and stepped into Tony's command center. "So what's this opportunity?"

Tony's eyes darted around the room before he continued, his voice barely above a whisper. "We got a few things goin' on 'round here, you know, behind the scenes? And you can benefit from it if you play your cards right. I know money is tight for you right now."

Jake raised an eyebrow. "You're a no-bullshit guy, Tony. So let's cut to the chase. Is it legal?"

"Get down off your high horse, kid," Tony scoffed. "Jigglin' your junk in public ain't exactly legal, neither, but we got you covered. So to speak."

"May I sit?" Jake asked, gesturing to an empty chair.

Tony grabbed a rag and tossed it to him. "Put this down under your sweaty butt, first."

Jake chuckled, spread the rag over the chair, and sat down slowly. "So what's the deal?"

A smile tugged at the corners of Tony's lips. "Trust me, kid, it's worth the risk."

Jake's thoughts raced as he considered the risks. *My college education? My future job prospects? My family? My reputation? Is it worth jeopardizing all of that?* But all he said was, "Okay, shoot."

"This, my friend, is foolproof," Tony assured him. "You'll be drivin' an inconspicuous pickup with fake tags."

Jake crossed his arms and let out a weary sigh. "And then what?"

"You'll drive to a prearranged location, they'll unload the cargo, and you drive away. Simple as that."

"That's it?" Jake's skepticism lingered.

"Easy peasy, right?" Tony replied, his fingers brushing together in satisfaction. "You won't even have to touch nothin'. You don't even get out of the truck."

As Tony's words hung in the air, Jake felt a knot tighten in his stomach. The realization washed over him like a cold wave. Was this simply Tony's under-the-table side hustle, or was the club a front for the mob?

Jake leaned back in his chair, the heaviness of the decision pressing on his shoulders. "Tony," he began, "I've got to be honest with you."

"You turnin' this down?" Tony took a deep breath and then exhaled. "You turnin' *me* down?"

"The offer is tempting," Jake said, "and, yes, I can certainly use the extra cash, but I can't take that risk, Tony. My head's about to explode from what I have on my plate as it is."

Tony's eyes held a glint of understanding mixed with disappointment. He let out a sigh, acknowledging Jake's stance. "I get it, kid. I know it's a lot."

The tension in the air was suffocating, and it left Jake with a sinking feeling that he might have damaged his relationship with Tony, a guy who believed in him and gave him an opportunity when he was desperate.

"I'm really sorry," Jake said.

Tony forced a smile. "Look, you're a good kid. I'm not holdin' it against you, okay? There'll be other opportunities down the road. No hard feelings. I'll get one of the other boys, but I came to you first because of your innocent face, right?"

Jake felt grateful for his understanding. "I appreciate that, Tony. And I promise I'll keep giving my all here at the bar."

Tony nodded. "That's what I like to hear. Now, get your sweaty rump back on stage. We got a crowd to please."

Jake headed to the door and halted. "Can I ask you one question?"

"Of course."

"What's on the truck?"

"I can't tell you that."

"How much does it pay?"

"That's *two* questions." Tony shook his head. "And I can't tell you that either, kid."

"Okay," Jake said. "Thanks, again, Tony."

"But I *can* tell you that you're makin' a big mistake," Tony's eyes narrowed. "Just so you know."

A chill ran down Jake's spine. Was the scared little voice inside him a warning that the next offer might not be so easy to refuse?

15. Who's the Boss?

IN THE main dining room of the most exclusive Italian restaurant in the heart of the city, the whispers about Max Marino swirled like smoke from a freshly lit cigar. The city's most notorious mob boss remained a figure of dark legend, an aging enigma whose shadowy presence cast a long, chilling aura over his criminal empire.

"Why don't you buy this place, Max?" asked his lunch companion, Detective Danny O'Neal. "It's a fuckin' gold mine, and you owning it would keep it from falling into the wrong hands."

Max shook his head as he stuffed a chunk of Italian bread into his mouth. "Don't shit where you eat. You never heard that?"

"Yeah, I heard it," the detective said, laughing. "It never crossed my mind, though, with this bein' a restaurant and all."

Max washed the bread down with a slug of Chianti. "That's 'cause yer a dumb Mick," he mumbled.

Max Marino was a bloated figure stuffed into an expensive suit two sizes too small, his scarred, hawk-like face a roadmap of his ruthless journey through the underworld. Born into a world of poverty and desperation, he learned early that life would show no mercy. He cut his teeth in the streets, where the echoes of gunfire were the lullabies of his youth. It was in the concrete jungle that he honed his survival instincts, where the only rule that mattered was that there were no rules, and Max, well, he soon made his own.

But he wasn't merely your garden variety brute. He was a shrewd strategist, a puppeteer who knew when to pull the strings and when to cut them. His empire thrived not only because of his muscle, but because of his mind. Max had a keen sense for opportunity and an unwavering resolve to seize it. His criminal enterprises spanned from gambling dens to smuggling routes and from counterfeit operations to protection rackets. No one could doubt the breadth of his ambition and the depth of his influence.

Loyalty was Max's code, the blood that ran through the veins of his criminal family. He demanded it like a collector of rare gems. His inner circle was a tight-knit group of individuals who had sworn allegiance to him, understanding that betrayal meant death. And in the world of Max Marino, death was often a slow and painful experience.

Max signaled to the waiter. "How's the calamari today, Sal?"

"Excellent, Mr. Marino," the waiter said, scraping and bowing. "Prepared just the way you like it, sir."

Max handed him back the menu. "Okay, then, bring me some of that. And more bread."

"Yes, sir," the waiter said, lowering his head with respect.

"More wine, too," Max added.

"Certainly, sir."

"So how's Veronica these days?" asked the detective.

"She's still a cunt," Max growled. "If she had as many cocks stickin' outta her as she's had stuck in her, she'd look like a fuckin' porcupine."

The wide-eyed detective appeared shocked. "You let her get away with that crap?"

"Better than me fuckin' her." Max tore off a hunk of bread and slathered it with butter. "She can't get knocked up no more, so who gives a big greasy shit?"

"What happened to that strict loyalty code of yours?" asked the detective.

"It don't apply to her," Max said with a mouthful. "Unless she starts screwin' somebody works for me. Then I cut his dick and balls off and jam 'em down *her* throat."

"That reminds me, Maxie." The detective took a deep breath. "We found Louie Ricci's sausage and eggs because somebody mailed 'em to us, but what happened to the rest of that motherfucker?"

"How would I know?" Max said with a poker face.

A breach in Max's strict code of loyalty may not have applied to Mrs. Marino, but the rules were different for those in his inner business circle. One of the most shocking incidents in Max's criminal past had become a whispered legend among the few who dared to speak of it. It involved one of Max's most trusted lieutenants, Louie "Two-Times" Ricci.

Louie had been Max's right-hand man for years, a man who had committed countless acts of violence and crime in Max's name. He was a faithful and loyal servant, or so it appeared. But power, well, it has a way of twisting even the most steadfast loyalties.

One fateful night, the city's police force was closing in on Max's operations. Pressure was mounting from all sides, and it was clear someone had been leaking information to the authorities. Max, the strategist, could see through the veil of deceit, and his icy gaze fell on Louie. Suspicion was not enough for Max. He needed proof.

In a secret meeting held in the depths of an abandoned warehouse, Max confronted Louie. The two men locked eyes, and in that moment, the world held its breath. The betrayal was undeniable. Max had uncovered Louie's double-dealing, his secret alliance with a rival gang, and his willingness to hand over Max in exchange for power and protection.

Without uttering a word, Max nodded to his two bodyguards, who seized Louie and tied him naked to a rusted steel chair. What followed involved a pair of bolt cutters, and it was said that even the most hardened mobsters who had witnessed the horror could barely keep their stomachs from turning. Max, a man who valued loyalty above all else, showed no mercy to the traitor in his midst, and his gruesome end served as a chilling testament to Max Marino's unwavering resolve that betrayal carried a price far too heavy to pay.

"Where the fuck is my calamari?" Max said, craning his neck to scan the restaurant. "I'll have that fuckin' waiter's *testicoli* for dessert."

16. Swirl

IN A world obsessed with fame, wealth, and success, the privileged elite reign supreme, and Benjamin Mendelsen was no exception. Ben had always been cushioned by a life of affluence and opulence. His parents, successful investors, saw to it that their son was provided for in every way. They financed his education, bought him expensive clothes, and raised him to freely explore life's pleasures.

Ben possessed an air of confidence and charisma that drew people to him. Men were attracted by the allure of recklessness, and his ne'er-do-well bad-boy boyishness made him the quintessential ladies' man. He reveled in the attention and sought out the instant gratification of relationships as fleeting as the fall leaves on the college campus grounds.

It was during his sophomore year that the initial spark had been ignited during a spring break trip to Las Vegas with his friends. With his dad's credit card tucked securely in his wallet, he had ventured into the gaudy, neon-lit casinos that adorned the city, a decadent Pleasure Island like in *Pinocchio*.

As Ben stepped onto the casino floor, the chiming of the slot machines, the spinning of the roulette wheels, and the luxurious sea of green felt tables intoxicated him. The high-rolling gamblers, clad in tuxedos, and the scantily clad babes supplying free cocktails fueled his desire to take part in the thrill. A dormant beast had awakened inside him, yearning for the adrenaline rush gambling promised.

With a few lucky spins at the roulette table, Ben doubled his initial bet. The triumph, the admiration of onlookers, and the hypnotic allure of winning hooked him instantly.

Ben stood in the center of the bustling casino, the glittery surfaces reflecting off his youthful face as he watched the roulette wheel spin. The clattering of chips and the excited chatter of the crowd filled the room. He felt a sexual surge as the white ball danced along the spinning wheel, finally settling into a slot: Red 14.

The cheers erupted from the crowd, and Ben couldn't help but grin. He had placed his bet on Red 14, and it had paid off handsomely. His stack of chips had doubled. He looked around, soaking in the admiration of onlookers, many of whom were envious of his lucky streak.

A middle-aged man in a flashy suit leaned over and slapped Ben on the back. "You're on fire, kid. Keep it up, and you'll be going home a rich man."

Ben nodded, trying to hide his growing excitement. "It's been a wild night so far, bro."

He watched the croupier spin the wheel again, and this time he chose to bet on odd numbers. As the ball settled into Black 9, Ben's winning streak continued. His chip stack grew, and the excitement in the casino intensified as a crowd gathered around him.

A pretty young woman leaned in closer to him, her eyes glittering with admiration. "You've got some serious luck on your side tonight, sweetie. You busy later?"

Ben chuckled, feeling invincible. "Catch me after I break the bank, baby," he said, giving her a hug.

The young woman pulled a few chips from her handbag and placed them next to Ben's on the table. As they watched the wheel spin, their eyes widened as the ball landed on Red 17, their chosen number. She squealed with delight and jumped up to kiss Ben full on the lips.

"Beginner's luck," she laughed, raking in her winnings.

As the night wore on, Ben's streak showed no signs of slowing down. He kept doubling his money with every successful spin, and the crowd around the table continued to grow. People were drawn to his charisma, his unending luck, and the intoxicating allure of winning. The chips piled up in front of him, a pyramid of success.

"You're a legend, buddy." a young man exclaimed. "I've never seen anything like this. What's your secret?"

Ben shrugged, his modesty barely concealing his excitement. "Just going with my gut. I guess tonight's my night."

The roulette wheel spun again, and this time, Ben's luck took a slight turn. The ball settled in the dreaded Green 0, causing him to lose a substantial amount of his winnings. The room fell silent for a moment, and Ben's heart sank. He could feel the weight of the loss. Then he shook off the disappointment and placed another bet. "No worries, folks. I got this."

The wheel spun once more, and this time, Red 23 came to his rescue. The crowd erupted into cheers, and Ben's smile returned, brighter than ever.

The pretty young woman put her arm around Ben's waist, a glint of seduction in her eyes. "You're not just lucky, you're unshakeable."

As the night wore on, Ben continued to place his bets, guided by intuition and luck. An older man turned to Ben, a drink in his hand. "You remind me of a guy I met here years ago. Kept winning big and then disappeared. You planning on sticking around, or is this your one-night wonder?"

Ben hesitated for a moment, the allure of winning pulling him in. But he looked around at the beaming faces of his newfound friends and then back at the older man, and a feeling of level-headedness settled over him. "I'm going to play it safe, man. I've had a great night, and I think I should quit while I'm ahead, don't you?"

The older man nodded and winked. "Smart move, kid. Enjoy your winnings."

Ben cashed out his chips and skipped out of the casino with his pockets stuffed with bills. The pretty young woman followed him out to the sidewalk and grabbed his arm. "You want some company tonight, handsome?"

"Thanks, baby, but I'm gonna sleep all alone and buck naked on top of all this *moolah*," he said with a mile-wide killer grin.

He stood under the marquee of the Bellagio and inhaled the smell of desert night air, the smell of car exhaust, and the smell of money. The busy swirl of the flashing, dashing, and racing neon displays on the Vegas Strip hypnotized him. Time had come for him to retreat to the quiet of his hotel room and count his stash.

As he crossed the street and walked towards his hotel, his fingers toyed with the lump of bills in his jacket pocket. He stopped dead in his tracks and appeared to go into a trance until the angry horn from a taxi cab brought him back to reality.

Ben made an about-face and stared at the blinking lights above the Bellagio and felt the physical pull of the allure of the roulette table inside.

"Fuck it," he muttered to himself. "I'll only risk *half* of it."

17. Cheaters

MARCO Santangelo, bathed in the soft golden glow of the bedside lamp, stared up at the ornate hotel room ceiling, deep in thought. Beads of sweat glistened on his tanned skin, the damp satin sheets beneath him a testament to the passion that had so recently ignited the room.

He was born into a working-class Italian-American family, raised by a single mother who was never quite sure who Marco's father was. His talent for dance became apparent at a young age, and although money was tight, his mother scrimped to pay for dance lessons. He started working as a bartender when he turned twenty-one, which led him eventually to transition from pouring drinks to performing on the club's stage. His exotic looks and sensual dance moves made him the star attraction at The Velvet Joystick, that is, until Jake Whitney's candy-ass appeared on the horizon.

Veronica rolled over and propped herself up on one elbow, her long hair cascading over her bare shoulders. "A penny for your thoughts," she said, her voice soft and husky.

Marco rolled onto his stomach to look at her, taking in the sight of her naked body. She was twice his age, but still stunningly beautiful. "I'm just trying to figure out what we're doing here," he said, still trying to catch his breath.

"It's called *fucking*," Veronica purred. "I believe it was invented by the Phoenicians somewhere in central Ohio around the turn of the century."

"I mean, we can't keep doing this forever, right?" Marco asked, his tone anxious. "Your husband is a dangerous man, Ronnie, and if he finds out about us, he'll kill me. He'll kill *us*."

Veronica reached out and traced an elegantly manicured finger down the crack of his backside. "I know," she said, her voice filled with longing. "But I can't help how I feel about you, Marco. You make me feel so alive."

Marco sighed, knowing her magnetic pull was powerful. "We have to be careful," he said. "We can't let anyone find out about us."

Veronica nodded, her expression desperate. "No kidding, baby," she said. "But I don't want to let you go. I *can't* let you go."

They laid for a few moments, each lost in their own thoughts. Marco knew he was playing a dangerous game, but he couldn't fight off Veronica's allure. She was intoxicating, and she made him feel alive, too, even though he knew at any moment it could all come crashing down around him.

"I have to admit," he sighed, "the sex is phenomenal."

"I think I love you," Veronica whispered, her eyes filled with longing.

"You *think*?" Marco closed his eyes, the words bringing a rush of emotion washing over him. Was Veronica more than a fling? He knew he could easily love her, even though they had only known each other for a few weeks.

Veronica hesitated. "Don't ask for the moon when we have the stars." She got up to search for her clothes, which were strewn about the room.

"Huh?" he said, getting drowsy.

"It's from some corny old movie," she sighed. "The kind of movie they made way before you were born."

Marco sat up and put his feet on the floor. "So this wham-bam hotel room stuff is all this is ever going to be?"

Holding her underwear, she slid next to Marco on the bed. "You brought a spark back into my life, baby, that I haven't felt in years, and I don't want to lose you, but I can't give Max up either."

"Yeah, I know," Marco said, flopping backward on the bed. "A cement overcoat would clash with my eyes."

Veronica giggled and threw her underwear aside to straddle him. "How about one more round for the road?"

Marco patted a yawn. "I'm having trouble staying awake, Ronnie."

"I can't imagine why," she laughed. "You pumped the life out of both of us."

"Why don't we stay here together tonight?" he asked. "Then when my batteries are recharged..."

Veronica nibbled on her bottom lip and shrugged. "You can stay if you want. Check-out is noon tomorrow, and it's paid for."

"Without you?"

"You know I don't like to linger afterwards." She pouted and stroked his face. "And Max will wonder where I am." She gave Marco a gentle kiss, then climbed off him and stepped into her dress.

"You keep pulling me back in," he said.

"What's that supposed to mean?" she snapped, her expression intense. "Are you thinking of leaving me?"

"This can't go on forever." He looked at her with concern in his eyes.

"I'm not losing you, Marco." Her gaze hardened. "You're a drug I can't quit."

After Veronica had gone, Marco lay tangled in the sheets and felt his heart pound as he grasped the gravity of his situation. He had spiraled into a world of desire, power, and danger, and he couldn't see a way out.

18. Advances

ETHAN sat alone in the dingy dressing room, nervously fidgeting with the edge of his g-string. The club's raucous music thudded through the walls, a stark contrast to the silence that enveloped him now. The dressing room smelled of sweat, hair product, and the subtle scent of Jake, who was busy on stage captivating the audience with his grace, charm, and drop-dead gorgeous looks. Ethan's eyes were fixed on his reflection in the mirror, trying to summon the courage he needed. "Why don't I look like him?" he murmured to himself.

As the minutes ticked away, Jake's performance ended, and the crowd's applause echoed through the backstage area. Ethan's heart raced knowing Jake would be back there soon, and it was only the two of them working the club tonight. He had spent months watching from the shadows, admiring Jake's every move, both on and off the stage. He had felt an inexplicable connection to him, something deeper than mere attraction.

The dressing room door creaked open, and there stood Jake, sweat glistening on his chiseled chest. His captivating eyes met Ethan's, and for a moment, it felt like time stood still.

"Hey," Jake said, his voice soft and inviting. "You ready to knock 'em dead, buddy?"

Ethan loved the way Jake called him 'buddy'. His mouth went dry, but he managed to croak out, "You already knocked 'em dead, buddy."

"You always know the perfect thing to say." Jake grabbed a towel and rubbed it over his body.

Ethan forced himself to speak, "Jake, there's something I need to tell you."

Jake turned to face him. "Sure, man. What's up?"

Ethan took a deep breath. "Well..." He didn't know if he could go on.

"You're looking a little lost there, buddy. What's on your mind?" Jake asked him.

Ethan's hands trembled as he tried to find the right words. "I... I've been watching you for a while, and it's not just because you're an incredible dancer..."

Tony barged into the room at that moment snorting like a bull ready to charge. He pointed an accusing finger at Jake. "So how come no cock and balls tonight?"

Jake threw his head back in frustration. "I wasn't in the mood tonight, okay?"

"You promised at least once a night, kid." Tony crossed his arms in front of his chest and waited for a reason.

"Is it that important?" Jake asked.

Tony brought his voice down to a whisper. "The word has spread that total nudity is on the menu at The Velvet Joystick. There's no turnin' back now."

Jake turned to Ethan. "Have you taken out the goods yet, buddy?"

"They all have, Jake, but it's just the two of you tonight," Tony said. "And Ethan, well, he's just not built like you." He glanced at Ethan "No offense meant."

"None taken," Ethan said. "I can't help it if I'm hung like a chipmunk."

"Don't let anyone intimidate you, buddy." Jake tapped Ethan on the shoulder. "Your package is just dandy."

"You think?" Ethan said smiling.

"Alright, alright, youse two. Get a room!" Tony stabbed a finger at Jake. "The junk comes out tomorrow," he shouted, and stormed out of the room.

Furious, Jake slapped the wet towel hard against the bench. With his back to Ethan, he bent over and slid his thong to the floor, his perfect backside no more than a foot from Ethan's face. Ethan shivered and lost all sense of decorum and control. He placed the palm of his trembling right hand flat against Jake's left butt cheek.

Jake lurched and spun around, falling against the wall. "What the fuck!"

Ethan jumped up in a panic. "I'm sorry, I'm sorry, I'm sorry." His voice quivered, and he was practically in tears.

Suddenly conscious of his nudity, Jake wrapped a towel around his waist. "What the heck are you doing, man?"

"I'm attracted to you, Jake. More than I can put into words." Ethan turned away in shame. "I've been struggling with this feeling for so long. Since the day we met."

The room shrank as the weight of Ethan's confession hung in the air. The silence was unbearable, and what he feared the most had, in fact, happened: Rejection.

Jake stared at him, his expression a mix of shock and understanding. He approached Ethan and placed a gentle hand on his shoulder. "I...I really appreciate your honesty, okay? It takes courage to share something like that."

Ethan's heart pounded in his chest, and he couldn't bring himself to meet Jake's gaze. "I'm so stupid."

Jake lifted Ethan's chin with his fingers, forcing him to look into those enchanting eyes of his. "I'm flattered that you feel this way about me. But, I have to be honest too. I'm not... I'm not *gay*. I hope you can understand."

Ethan's heart sank, and tears welled up in his eyes, and he struggled to keep them from spilling over. "Now we can't be friends anymore."

Jake's grip on Ethan's shoulder tightened, and he spoke with sincerity, "Ethan, our friendship means a lot to me. I don't want this to change anything between us. We can still be friends, okay?"

Ethan nodded, and Jake gave him a warm smile, pulling him into a tight hug. Ethan jerked away and struggled to speak. "Please...don't," he said, his eyes red and swollen. "When you touch me I just fall apart."

Tony's footsteps could be heard coming down the hall. Ethan wiped his tears away with the back of his hand and ran into the bathroom.

"Where the hell is chipmunk dick?" Tony growled.

Jake rolled his eyes. "Words can hurt, Tony."

"I'm just jokin' 'bout what he said." Tony threw up his arms. "What are youse two, a couple of *women*?"

"He's in the bathroom," Jake said, staring at the floor.

"Well, tell him he's on in *five*." Tony held up five fingers and wiggled them above his head as he stormed out again. "Jesus Christ! I'm runnin' a freakin' kinny-garten here."

19. The Management

THE harsh overhead lights flickered to life as Tony Gaudio pushed open the heavy storage room door carrying a case of long-necked Heinekens. He had been running the establishment for close to a decade, and each night still held a unique promise, as well as a lurking fear.

As the manager of The Velvet Joystick, Tony's days were a whirlwind of chaos and contrast. His mornings usually began with a flurry of phone calls to order beer and booze and handle last-minute emergencies. Max Marino, the mob boss who owned the club, didn't tolerate any slip-ups. Tony had seen the results of Max's wrath enough times to know perfection was the only option.

A man of rugged charm who never spoke of family or anyone close, Tony's tough, street-wise face gave him an authoritative presence. His daily attire typically consisted of a crisp dress shirt, suspenders, and well-fitted trousers, portraying a professional image even in a casual bar setting.

With a strong espresso in hand, Tony would spend his afternoons managing the club's finances, juggling bills and counting the dwindling stacks of cash from the previous night's debauchery. Keeping the club afloat in an industry notorious for both glamour and fiscal instability was a constant challenge.

By early evening, after a quick dinner, Tony would make his way back to the club to prepare for the night's event. The dancers, a mix of egos and insecurities, could be a minefield of attitudes that Tony had learned to gingerly navigate. Their nerves were as shaky as their genitals, and he'd grown adept at massaging egos, providing pep talks, and, on occasion, issuing a stern warning when necessary to keep them in line.

Tony faced a particularly thorny situation with Brett Booth, one of his best dancers and a guy who seemed pretty normal and who minded his own business, unless he had a cause rattling around in his head. His

75

sculpted physique and seductive charisma made him an audience draw, but his demanding temperament often made Tony reach for the Tums.

Brett leaned against the bar, glaring at Tony with smoldering intensity. "I told you, Tony, I won't go on unless you repaint the stage floor and freshen up the dressing area. It's bad enough we have to change in front of each other with no privacy at all."

"Privacy? Whaddaya talkin' privacy? You shake your fruit basket in front of a hundred women each night." Tony barked, his frustration apparent. "Brett, we're all tryin' our best here, okay? You know how things are. The club can't afford it right now."

"It was me who booked that bachelorette party for next week," Brett said. "And my girl is coming, too. I don't want her to see me working in a dump." Brett's gaze didn't waver. "Fix up the joint, Tony. You owe me one."

Tony massaged his temples, the tension in his neck radiating down his spine. Dealing with Brett's diva-like demands was a chore, but Tony understood his importance to the club's bottom line. "Look, I'll see what I can do. But don't pull this on me every week, Brett. We're in this together."

As Tony navigated the egos and challenges of the dancers, his fears loomed in the background. Max Marino cast a menacing shadow over The Velvet Joystick. Tony had been in Max's employ since he'd opened the club, and Max's chilling past history was enough to keep him awake at night.

Max Marino had a reputation for brutality and ruthlessness that extended far beyond the city's limits. He demanded absolute loyalty from his employees, and in return, he offered protection for the club. But the price of that protection was steep, and Tony had seen what happened to those who dared to defy Max Marino.

It was Max who dictated the club's policies, Max who set the dancer's pay scale, Max who skimmed a generous portion of the club's profits, leaving Tony to manage on a shoestring budget. Tony had heard rumors of rival clubs where managers had disappeared without a trace, and he knew crossing Max could lead to a fate worse than death.

As the night's performances began, Tony stood in the shadows watching the dancers captivate the audience with their provocative moves. The room was bathed in a sultry ambiance, and the intoxicating blend of fear, frustration, and desire coursed through him.

Tony Gaudio had grown accustomed to the dual life he led, managing a world of sin and sensuality while dancing on the razor's edge of Max Marino's ruthless grip. Each night, he hoped The Velvet Joystick would continue to shine, his dancers would dazzle, and he could keep Max at bay, even if only for one more night.

20. Mad About the Boy

VERONICA Marino leaned against the hotel room's balcony railing, her eyes fixed on the bustling city below. The lights of downtown shimmered like a sea of stars, their glow casting a soft, sexy ambiance in the room. The scent of roses filled the air, and the gentle jazz playing in the background added to the romantic atmosphere.

Inside, the mood was set, but the atmosphere was far from relaxed. Veronica's guest, Jake Whitney, shifted from foot to foot. He'd never been in such an opulent place, and the situation was way out of his comfort zone.

"Jake, darling, relax," Veronica purred, sauntering over to him. She was stunning in her crimson evening gown, her hair cascading over her shoulders with her diamond necklace sparkling under the soft lighting.

Jake felt a knot form in his stomach. He was torn between his curiosity about this enigmatic woman and the uncertainty of the unknown. But the magnetic pull he felt was impossible to resist. He swallowed hard, his eyes darting around the room. "I... I can't help it. I've never been to a place like this. Your husband doesn't know, right?"

Veronica's gaze held a mix of affection and trepidation. "Of course not. He's out of town for business, anyway. Tonight, it's just you and me."

Jake exhaled slowly, trying to steady his racing heart. He glanced at the elegantly set table where a feast of exotic dishes awaited them. "I've never seen food like this before, either. What is all this?"

Veronica's lips curled into a knowing smile. "It's an Italian-Moroccan fusion. I thought you might enjoy something different. Please, have a seat."

As they sat down, she poured a glass of Chablis for each of them. Jake took a tentative sip, the wine's rich flavor new to his palate. He looked at the array of dishes before him, foreign ingredients and vibrant colors clashing with his humble background.

"You have, uh, *exquisite* taste," he mumbled, mustering a faint smile.

Veronica chuckled, tracing her fingers across the stem of her wine glass. "I wanted tonight to be special, Jake. You deserve a break from the daily grind. Is that an appropriate word? Grind?" She laughed.

"It is," he said, as his eyes met hers, and he managed a grateful smile. "I appreciate this. You're very kind."

The remaining moments were tense, each bite of food a mixture of complex flavors and anxiety. Veronica and Jake exchanged stolen glances, their chemistry undeniable. As they finished the meal, they shared dessert, a sweet Moroccan pastry that symbolized the forbidden nature of their connection.

With their meal concluded, Jake rose from the table. "Thank you for tonight," he whispered. "I have an early class tomorrow. Eight a.m."

"School, school, school," Veronica sighed, picking up his wine glass and slinking toward him. "You are not to waste a drop of this very expensive vintage." She handed him his glass, and as he put his head back to swallow the last of the wine, Veronica unbuckled the belt on his pants.

Jake's breath caught in his throat as she reached into his boxers and stroked him, her mouth trailing kisses down his neck. The rush of adrenaline mixed with desire was something he had never experienced before.

Veronica wasted no time in undressing Jake, her hands roaming over his toned, firm young body and the graze of her fingers on his skin made his testicles tighten.

Jake's mind went blank as Veronica took control. She grabbed his hand, guided him into the bedroom and pushed him onto the bed. They both laughed when they spotted the wine glass still gripped in his hand. Before Jake knew what hit him, Veronica had unzipped her crimson dress, stepped out of it, and climbed on top of him. *This woman is dangerous*, he thought, *insatiable, raw, and intense*. He realized it was useless to do anything but give in to the pleasure, and, alas, they both let go in a pulsating torrent of ebb and flow.

After a quiet respite of coming back to earth, Jake caught himself drifting off. He jumped up with a start, and, as Veronica watched him, dressed quickly, the sudden weight of guilt heavy on his shoulders. "This was nice," he whispered.

"Nice?" she growled. "This was nice like the eruption of Vesuvius was nice."

They arranged to leave the hotel room separately, doing their best to appear as if they were never together.

Jake slipped out first, swallowing deep gulps of air as he made his way down the street, every fiber in his body, from his toes to the hair on his head, tingling.

Veronica waited a few minutes before following. Back on the balcony, the city lights had lost their allure as she gazed into the dark abyss of the city streets below. She smiled as she recalled the advice her mother had given her when she first showed an interest in boys. "Marry for love, sweetie," she told her. "They all do the same thing in bed."

• • • •

21. Spotlight on Leo Shaw

LEO Shaw was not your typical young male dancer. By day, he toiled away at a monotonous job in a nondescript dollar store. But when the sun dipped below the horizon, and the city's neon lights flickered to life, Leo's true passion came alive. And no, it wasn't stripping.

Born to a family of mathematicians and engineers, Leo's desire to perform was an anomaly. His parents, Judy and Nelson Shaw, had always envisioned their son following in their footsteps. They'd saved for his college education, expecting him to pursue a practical career, but Leo's heart was set on the stage.

With his days spent at the dollar store, and his evenings strutting his stuff at The Velvet Joystick, any other moments he managed to squirrel away he dedicated to writing comedy material for a stand-up routine. It was a secret aspiration, one he knew his parents would not understand. They had never seen the allure in comedy and would consider it a frivolous pursuit.

Leo's apartment, a cramped studio in a somewhat rundown building, bore witness to his double life. Dance shoes and costumes mingled with notebooks filled with witty one-liners and comedic observations. In the early hours of the morning, he'd scribble down jokes while sipping his coffee, and when he came home exhausted and drained from a night of stripping, he would still take time before bed to practice his comedy routines in front of a dusty full length mirror.

His comedy idols were a diverse bunch. George Carlin's biting social commentary appealed to his desire to question societal norms. Eddie Murphy's energetic performances lit a fire within him, while Ellen DeGeneres' storytelling abilities made her a source of inspiration. And then there was Robin Williams, whose boundless energy and ability to morph into countless characters mesmerized Leo. He admired how they could bring joy, provoke thought, and offer an escape from the mundane. Making the world laugh was to Leo a noble profession.

Juggling his life as a dancer, a dollar store employee, and a budding comedian was no small feat. The dollar store job was a necessity, allowing him to pay the bills and keep his artistic pursuits a secret from his parents. He'd smile as he rang up customers' purchases, all the while mentally fine-tuning his jokes and routines. The job, though dull, was a well-disguised opportunity to observe people and gather material for his stand-up gigs.

Leo's performances at The Velvet Joystick had become a remote control thing. He found himself merely going through the motions, although he had refined his craft enough to still move with grace and passion, evoking emotions that were locked away during his daytime grind selling things for a buck.

On his off nights from the strip club he would rush to comedy clubs for open mic nights where he'd deliver his freshly minted jokes, hoping to catch the attention of an agent who might secure him a full-time gig.

Comedy audiences were, for the most part, unforgiving, and it didn't take long to figure out you were laying an egg. But it taught him the value of resilience, endurance, and timing, and knowing when to pause for laughter or press on in the face of silence.

He got in the habit of thumbing through the show business trade papers, hunting for auditions and opportunities. While he found a few one-night stands that paid a pittance, most auditions were met with rejection, a fact he'd kept from his parents. They remained blissfully unaware of their son's double life, and he wanted to keep it that way. Telling dumb jokes and getting naked in public we're not in Mom and Dad's DNA.

The strain of living this double life began to wear on Leo. He was exhausted, both physically and emotionally, as he balanced his day job, dance practice, and comedy gigs. There were moments of self-doubt, when he questioned if his pursuit of comedy would ever take off and whether it was worth the toll it took on his personal life, which was non-existent. The pawing and fondling he submitted himself to each night at The Velvet Joystick had been the extent of intimacy in his life for longer than he cared to remember.

However, every time Leo stepped onto a stage, whether as a dancer or a comedian, he felt truly alive. It was in those moments that he knew he was on the right path, and he couldn't turn back. With the feet of a dancer and the heart of a comedian, he was determined to chase his dreams, one step and one punchline at a time.

22. Designing Woman

"WILL the performance be *tasteful*?" Sarah made quotation marks with her fingers.

"Tasteful?" Brett's eyebrows wrinkled, and his forehead creased. "It's a strip club, hon. Guys twirl their *boy parts* and women lick their lips and throw money at them. Isn't that the basic recipe for a bachelorette party?"

From their booth inside the Cosmic Coffee Shop, Sarah gazed out the window at the bustling early morning rush hour traffic and started to stress. "I'm having second thoughts," she said.

"*Now* you're having second thoughts?" Brett replied, over-stirring his coffee. "The shindig is Saturday night."

Sarah Miller thought of herself as having impeccable taste and attention to detail. Her life was a carefully curated space filled with neutral colors, clean lines, and an air of sophistication. She loved nothing more than transforming ordinary spaces into extraordinary works of art. Okay, so maybe she didn't love it more than she loved Brett Booth, her hunky exotic dancer boyfriend who swept her off her feet three months before at a Coldplay concert.

Everything going on in her life expanded in her head until she thought it would explode. The upcoming bachelorette party she had planned for her best friend, Amy, and the wedding to follow, was costing her more than she realized it would. Her designing position at Interior Motives kept her in perpetual motion all day, and sometimes into the night, with demands from her boss, her clients, her staff, and a constant barrage of emails, texts, and tweets. Then there was her opposites-attract-relationship with a male, let's-be-honest-here, *stripper*, who was perfectly content taking it all off nightly for a waistband full of cash.

Sarah turned away from the window and looked into Brett's gorgeous bedroom eyes. "Amy put her trust in me to find a suitable venue, and, don't get me wrong, Brett, you came to my rescue when all else failed."

He looked at her and nodded. "Yeah, but...?"

"Amy's mother will be there," she said. "And her grandma, too, who I doubt has ever seen a penis."

"After Saturday she still won't have seen a penis," he said. "Tony has ruled out the Full Monty at bachelorette parties because they're not usually regulars and he wants to be cautious and avoid any trouble that might result from complaints about public nudity. There's always one of those apples in the barrel."

"Well, at least that's something, anyway." Sarah relaxed a bit, but the anxiety of the situation still lingered in her mind. "What if something goes wrong? And what if Amy blames me for it?"

Brett put his hand on top of Sarah's and looked deep into her eyes. "Listen, hon. You've planned everything perfectly. The party is going to be amazing, and Amy is going to be thrilled. And when it's all said and done, her mother and grandmother will still love her, and you'll still be her best friend. It's going to be okay."

Sarah smiled, grateful for Brett's support. "Thanks, Brett. You always know how to make me feel better."

"Of course, babe. That's what I'm here for." Brett leaned in and kissed her. "And who knows, maybe you'll even have a little fun yourself."

Sarah rolled her eyes. "I doubt that. I don't think strip clubs are really my scene."

Brett laughed. "Well, you never know until you try."

Sarah had never been to a strip club before, but the more she thought about it, the more intrigued she became. Maybe it wouldn't be so bad after all.

As they finished their coffee and headed out onto the busy street, Brett wrapped his arm around her waist and pulled her close. She hoped the people passing by took notice of the *be-still-my-beating-*

heart-hunk-of-love that little Sarah Miller had been lucky enough to nab for herself.

23. The Bachelorette

THE day of the bachelorette party arrived, and Sarah found herself feeling a mix of nerves and excitement as she helped Amy get ready. They had rented a limousine to take the bride-to-be and her six attendants to the strip club, and Sarah couldn't help but feel a little intimidated as they pulled up to the gaudy looking lounge with the neon sign overhead bathing the sidewalk in shades of pink and purple. The bottle of peach schnapps Amy brought along did a great deal to mellow the mood.

As soon as they stepped inside the bar, they were greeted by loud music, swirling lights, and flowing drinks. Tony and the boys had pulled out all the stops to bring The Velvet Joystick up to a sophisticated level of raunchy fun. The interior was an explosion of color, with a freshly painted mirrored stage in the center.

Sarah was swept up in the atmosphere and found herself cheering along with the other women, laughing at the jokes, and even throwing a few bucks onto the stage herself. And when Brett's performance came up, she was bouncing in her seat with excitement. As he made his way onto the stage, she couldn't help but feel a surge of pride for her talented and sexy boyfriend. His moves were smooth and electrifying, and the way he interacted with the other women in the audience only added to his charm. Sarah found herself feeling grateful that she had someone like him in her life who could bring her so much joy and pleasure and smoking hot sex.

As Brett shed his clothing, Sarah felt her heart rate increase. She knew she loved him for more than his physique, but seeing him like this was a tantalizing reminder of the passion and sensuality they shared together. She watched with bated breath as he teasingly revealed more and more of his toned body, until he was left standing in nothing but a glittery gold thong.

The crowd erupted into cheers and applause, and Sarah found herself standing up and shouting his name along with the others. Brett looked out into the audience and caught her eye, giving her a bad-boy look. Amy turned to Sarah and shouted at the top of her voice, "Lucky *bitch*! You get to run your tongue all over that."

Sarah blew Brett a kiss as he left the stage, and her eyes landed on a shadowy figure preparing to perform in the background. When the spotlight hit him, she felt a cold shivering thrill, as if a ray of celestial light had streamed down from the heavens to highlight one glorious godlike creature. Everything else in the room went dim as he stepped onto the stage. And that was the first time Sarah laid eyes on Jake Whitney.

He was the epitome of boyish handsomeness, and she couldn't help but feel her heart rate increase as he moved his incredible body. His hips swayed to the music, and his muscles rippled with every beat. Sarah found herself completely unable to look away.

Jake couldn't help but feel drawn to Sarah's piercing expression as he gyrated on stage. Her shiny auburn hair and fresh natural beauty caught his attention. She could feel his gaze on her, too, and the intensity of it made her feel like she was on fire. As they locked eyes, Sarah felt a sudden jolt of electricity pass between them as if they were the only two people in the room.

As the music sputtered to its flashy finish and the stage lights faded, Jake's performance came to an end, and Sarah knew she wanted him. Then she recognized the hazy figure of Brett Booth toweling off in the distance, and she felt a flicker of guilt for her unfaithful fantasy.

After the performance, Brett introduced her to Jake. "He's one of our star performers here." Then he slapped himself on the forehead. "Well, duh, I guess you figured that out by now."

Jake extended his hand, a warm and genuine smile on his face. "Nice to meet you, Sarah. Brett's told me a lot about you."

Sarah shook his hand, feeling somewhat overwhelmed. "Likewise, Jake. Your performance was... well, it was...*mesmerizing*. I've never been to a place like this before."

"Well, welcome." Jake exclaimed. "And thank you. I try my best to keep the audience entertained. So, how's the bachelorette thing going tonight?"

"So far so *great*," Sarah said with a goofy giggle. "I'm a bridesmaid, and we thought this would be a fun idea."

"Um, excuse me." Brett interrupted. "*I* thought this would be a fun idea. Time to give credit where credit is due."

"You were right, honey," Sarah told him, pulling him closer. Then she turned to Jake. "He was right, okay?"

"Wow," Brett said. "I wish I had a recording of *that*."

Sarah nudged Brett with her elbow. "How about getting me a margarita?"

"Coming right up," Brett said. "Sugar around the rim, no salt, right?"

"He knows me so well," Sarah said, flashing an awkward thumbs up.

Jake watched Brett head to the bar. "Great guy."

"The best," Sarah agreed.

Jake leaned in, his lips hovering close to Sarah's ear as he whispered, "You're beautiful."

Sarah's heart skipped a beat, and she felt her cheeks flush with heat.

Amy staggered toward them from amongst the crowd, three sheets to the wind. "This is my last night to howl before I tie the knot around a life of misery." she slurred. "Man, I would give anything to get fucked here tonight."

"Now, what would Larry say if he heard you talk like that?" Sarah said.

"Fuck Larry," Amy said. "I can't believe that after next week, the only *cock* I'll ever get to suck belongs to dumpy old Larry."

Brett returned, carefully balancing Sarah's overfilled margarita. "Having fun, Amy?"

"Hell, yes!" she exclaimed. "All this prime beef so near and yet so far."

Sarah put her arm around Amy to hold her up. "I think maybe it's time to switch over to black coffee, Amy."

"I'm done for the night," Brett said. "So I'll help pile you gals into the car whenever you're ready."

"And I have to get ready for my next set," Jake said. "It was great meeting you, Sarah. I hope you survive the wedding next week."

Sarah watched Jake walk away and found it difficult to tear her eyes from him.

Brett hooked his thumbs into his waistband and rocked on his toes. "That's got me thinkin'," he said.

Sarah snapped to attention and looked at Brett with a silly grin. "Huh? What's got you thinking?"

"All this wedding talk is giving me ideas," he said.

"What sort of ideas?" she asked him, even though she knew the answer. For some reason, what he was hinting at filled her with an awful feeling of dread all of a sudden.

24. Pressure Point

MAX Marino's black Lincoln Town Car pulled up in front of The Velvet Joystick at exactly nine a.m. in the morning.

Tony had expected him, and he was waiting and ready when the mob boss walked through the front door about five feet behind his reputation, flanked by an armed bodyguard on each side. Tony rose to greet him and welcomed him to a table that had been set elegantly with a linen cloth and a crystal ashtray.

"I don't smoke no more since my *prostrate*," Max said, shoving the ashtray across the table and lowering himself on the chair.

"That footlong Cuban was your trade mark," Tony said with a patronizing chuckle.

"I need you to do somethin' for me," Max said in a voice that signaled the meeting was about business and business only, no pleasantries necessary.

Tony nodded. "Anything, boss."

Max surveyed the empty club. "So you got faggots workin' here, huh?"

"Faggots?" Tony was at a loss for a reply.

"*Poofy* boys...*fanook*...runnin' 'round bare-assed," he said, his wrist limp in case Tony didn't quite grasp the question. "Come on, Tony, you know what I'm talkin'."

"Nah," Tony said, waving the idea away. "All my boys here are straight arrows. They love women, which is why they're doin' this here. They love it when the bitches touch their junk, you know what I'm sayin', Maxie?"

Max threw his head back and croaked out a wheezing laugh, and the bodyguards did the same.

"I love it when bitches touch my junk, too, right?" Max let out another wheezer that broke down in a coughing fit, taking careful inventory to assure everyone else enjoyed his comic brilliance as much as he did. "But them days is long gone since it don't get hard no more."

"Sorry to hear that, Max," Tony said with great sympathy. "You were a legendary cocksman back in the day."

"Nothin' lasts forever, Tony, but small talk 'bout my pecker ain't why I'm here." He cleared his throat and took a breath. "I asked if they was faggots 'cause I'm lookin' for *real* men, ones with *steel* balls hangin' 'tween their legs, okay?"

"I hear ya, Max," Tony said. "So, for *why* are you lookin'?"

"I need for you to convince one or two of your footsie-tootsie boys, whatever you call 'em, to do some jobs for me on the side."

Tony frowned. "Like what, exactly?"

Max frowned, too, and storm clouds appeared overhead "What do *you* mean what do *I* mean?" He looked at his two henchmen and shrugged. Tony got the idea he hadn't asked a great question.

"Oh, okay, Max," Tony said, nodding. "I understand, I understand."

"I need 'em to help me out with my businesses," Max nodded. "Runnin' errands, deliverin' messages, collectin' debts, some drop offs maybe, that sort of thing. See my guys are too well known about the face, since bein' in and out of the slammer, you understand. Long story short, I need fresh faces that don't got no record."

The Ringling Brothers Circus moved into the center ring of Tony's head and was about to blow his brains out of a canon. Max was asking him to put his employees at risk, and if they got caught, they could go to jail, and even worse, Tony could go to jail, too.

"Will they get protection?" Tony asked.

"The only way they'll get protection, Tony, is if they go out and buy a box of rubbers," Max said. "A job is a job, and life is fulla risks. There's no guarantee you're gonna get away with nothin'. That's why I pay so good."

"So how much you payin'?" Tony asked.

"Depends on the job," Max said. "I'm sure they all can use the extra cash. If they was trust fund babies, they wouldn't be slavin' in this here shithole sellin' their cookies for a buck a pop. They might like workin' for me better, so you best be on your toes and watch your back, Tony."

"Max, I always watch my back," Tony said. "I'll talk to them tonight."

"I only need two," Max said, holding up two fingers. "At least to start. I'll have Bruno call you tomorrow for the names." Max waved for his two goons to help him up.

Tony ran ahead and opened the front door. "Nice to see you lookin' so well, Max."

Max gasped out another laugh. "Never bullshit a bullshitter, Tony."

25. Lucky Catch

"A RAGING success!"..."Best bachelorette bash ever!"..."I had the time of my life!"

Sarah poured over the effusive texts she had received from her fellow bridesmaids regarding the big event.

Brett kept stabbing the elevator button with increasing frustration. "Slowest damn elevator in the city."

Sarah waved her phone in front of Brett's face. "Did you hear anything I said?"

"Yes, yes," he said as the elevator door finally slid open. "I had to hear about that damn bachelorette party for weeks before it. Do I have to put up with it for weeks afterwards, too?"

When the door swung open on Sarah and Brett's one-bedroom efficiency apartment, the soft glow of their cozy living room welcomed them. As they slipped off their shoes and flopped on the sofa, Sarah stretched, yawned, and purred, "Home sweet home."

Brett looked over at her with eyes filled with affection for the woman he loved. "I'm so glad it worked out, though."

Sarah wasn't about to give up the afterglow. "The decor, the games, the music—everything was just perfect. But you know what made it even more sensational?"

Brett put his head back to rest his eyes. "My dance?" he said with a grin.

"*Jake Whitney*!" she exclaimed, her voice filled with enthusiasm.

Brett's eyes popped open, fully awake. "Huh?"

"What a charmer," she said, swooning. "I can't help but think that he played a big part in making the night so special."

Brett masked his discomfort with a forced smile. "Jake? Well, sure, he's a good guy. I'm glad you liked him."

Sarah was oblivious to Brett's unease. "He's not just *good*, Brett. He's *incredible*. So handsome and funny, and he kept everyone entertained. What a catch for some lucky girl, right?"

"Yeah, what a catch," he said, his heart sinking.

"Is he dating anyone?" she asked. "Do you know if he's single and available?"

"He doesn't share much with the rest of us," Brett told her.

Sarah sat up and meditated. "Mary Lou is still in a blue funk since Jason dumped her. This guy Jake would be the perfect cure for her heartbreak, don't you think?"

"Apparently you think he would be the cure for everything." Brett shook his head. "World hunger, maybe? How about...?"

Sarah interrupted him. "Why aren't you two closer friends?"

"Well," Brett said, rolling his eyes, "for starters, he's not my type."

"You know what I mean," she said, lightly punching his arm. "I think we should invite him over. Hey, we'll get Mary Lou to come, too. Matchmaker, matchmaker."

Brett's smile hardened into a strained one. "Sarah, I appreciate your enthusiasm, but I don't think we need to get involved in..."

"Why not?" She raised an eyebrow, clearly puzzled by Brett's reaction. "I just thought it would be great if my amazing boyfriend had a friend as amazing as he is, that's all."

Brett struggled to find the right words to express his discomfort. "It's just that, well, I'd rather focus on *us*, Sarah. I'm more interested in making our relationship stronger and planning our future together."

Her eyes narrowed. "Why? Don't we have a strong relationship now?"

"That's not what I meant."

Sarah reached for Brett's hand and squeezed it. "I'm making you uncomfortable. You're right, Brett. I love you, and I'm sorry for getting carried away. You're the most important person in my life, and nothing will ever change that."

Brett leaned in to kiss Sarah, their lips meeting in a sweet and reassuring moment. "That's all I want to hear, Sarah. I'm thrilled that you had a great time at the party, but remember, we're the ones who have something special. You and I. Let's cherish that."

As they cuddled on the couch, the warm ambiance of the room and their affection for each other filled the space. But Brett regretted not booking the bachelorette party at Chuck E. Cheese.

26. Conspicuous Consumption

MARCO rolled Veronica onto her stomach, enjoying her squeal of pleasure. They'd been going at it for over an hour and he wondered if she would ever have enough.

Then, as his heart thundered in his ribcage, he braced himself for the ultimate climax, and when he could no longer resist, there was a loud cry from both of them as if they had been riding a roller coaster that jumped the track, sending them into an eternal abyss with a sensation so thrilling that death hardly mattered.

Veronica shook and uttered "Oh, my God" over and over until they both collapsed in a pool of sticky sweat. Then her phone lit up on the bedside table and played the theme from *The Godfather.* "Fuck, fuck, *fuck,*" she said, pushing Marco away and crawling out from under him. "It's my husband." She grabbed for the phone and read the text message. "He's on his way up here!"

Marco jumped off the bed like he was on fire and scrambled to collect his scattered clothing, his erection fading from sixty to zero in a matter of seconds. "How does he even know you're here?" he exclaimed.

"Who knows what Max Marino knows?" she said. "That's the scary part of my life."

Marco put his undershorts on backwards, but he didn't care. "How do I get out of the building? What if he sees me?"

"Take the stairs down to the basement," she directed, "and go out by the loading dock."

"Something tells me you've done this before," Marco said, as he stuffed his socks into his pocket and put his shoes on over bare feet.

Veronica opened the hotel room door. "Hurry, hurry," she said, "and don't make eye contact with anyone."

Marco pecked her on the cheek, and she watched him sprint down the hall towards the stairway entrance. Closing the door behind him, she couldn't help but enjoy a good laugh. The fake-a-call feature on her phone had become her trusted ally. It allowed her to gracefully exit tedious conversations at parties, escape from people she found insufferable, and strike fear into young men terrified her gangster husband might discover where they were hiding the salami.

With a hint of mischief in her eyes, she knew she had a precious window of time to prepare for her next rendezvous. She quickly set about straightening the bed, washing her face, fixing her hair, and slipping into the luxurious La Perla silk robe she had purchased for the occasion. It was an exquisite garment with an opulent belt that required only an effortless tug to reveal the depth of her passion to her shiny new lover.

As she primped in front of the mirror, Veronica savored the intoxicating excitement her secret liaisons brought into her life. The thrill of stealthily navigating her affairs under Max's nose, all while maintaining her impeccable facade, added an irresistible element of danger to her pampered, but otherwise monotonous, life.

Her reflection in the mirror whispered stories of sin only she could hear. The sizzle of these illicit encounters, the tantalizing dance on the razor's edge, was a heady cocktail that Veronica had grown addicted to. It was as if every stolen moment was a rebellion against the constraints of her perfect existence.

In the soft glow of the vanity mirror, Veronica couldn't help but wonder how she had become this woman leading a double life, a life hidden in a world of desire and deception. She was a master at concealing her indiscretions, a virtuoso in the art of passion behind closed doors and a poised hostess at social gatherings.

Yet, as she applied a final touch of lipstick and smoothed the fabric on the robe, a pang of guilt tugged at her conscience. She had deceived herself into believing Max remained oblivious to her secret liaisons, and that she had actually been skillful in keeping her polished surface intact, and her marriage unscathed. But the risk, the thrill, and the magnetic pull of forbidden love swirled in a vortex she couldn't escape. Veronica reminded herself that this private world was the spice that made her life tolerable.

Her heart raced as she heard the faint knock at the door, signaling the young man's arrival. The anticipation of their stolen moments together was a drug she couldn't quit, and she knew that once she opened that door, she was diving headlong into the intoxicating, dangerous thrill that had become her obsession.

After a final check in the mirror, she swept to the door and pulled it open with a dramatic flourish. Jake Whitney stood tall in dress pants and open shirt holding a bouquet of flowers and looking like a prince from a fairy tale.

"I hope you like daisies," he said as Veronica pulled him into the room.

"I'd love anything you gave me," she said, placing her hand on his crotch. "Especially *this*."

27. Loan Shark

"SO, do you think this dude Max Marino would lend me some dough?" Ben was anxious, desperate, and at the end of his rope.

Jake stared at his roommate as if he had lost his fucking mind, then he said, "Have you lost your fucking mind?"

Ben shrugged. "Hey, you don't ask, you don't get."

"Right," Jake said. "And you don't pay, you don't breathe."

"Dude, I maxed my credit out to the tune of twenty thousand simoleons," Ben squealed. "My father gets the bill on the tenth of the month."

"Keep it down," Jake told him. "You're going to wake everyone in the dorm. We can't afford to get thrown out on our asses."

One would never have known that Ben Mendelsen's once-charmed existence lay crumbled in ruins. He attended classes with a facade of nonchalance, always impeccably dressed, and never revealing the financial turmoil lurking beneath his charismatic exterior. Daddy had stepped in to get him out of jams in the past, but this wanton lack of respect for money combined with a gambling addiction was not in the same league as when he got a girl pregnant in the summer between his sophomore and junior year. Daddy made it all go away - the pregnancy, the girl, and any sense of responsibility on Ben's part. But this latest *tumult* involved money, and that was like spitting on the Torah in the Mendelsen house.

"If I could just secure a loan for, say, five thousand bucks," Ben reasoned, "then I could make one big bet, win it all back, and *badabing*, I'd be home free."

Jake sat up in bed astonished by Ben's lack of common sense. "So your *numbskull* strategy is to do the exact same thing that got you into this mess in the first place."

Ben rolled over and lifted himself on one elbow. "How do you figure?"

'Okay, listen up," Jake said. "You owe twenty thousand, so if you borrow five more there's gonna be interest on that."

"There is?"

"Yes, *doofus*." Jake rolled his eyes. "Do you think an animal like Max Marino is gonna fork over 5K to you without there's something in it for him?"

"So how much interest you think he'll charge? Like maybe five percent?"

"This is the *mob* we're talking about, not Chase Manhattan." Jake threw his pillow at Ben. "You better figure fifty percent to be safe."

Ben sat bolt upright. "The fuck!"

"That means you have to win thirty thousand to pay off both Max Marino and your credit card debt." Jake got out of bed to get his pillow back and smack Ben in the head. "The oldest delusion in gambling is thinking all your problems would be solved by one massive win."

"I feel pretty confident, though," Ben said. "I worked out a system."

"And if you lose the five grand, then what?" Jake glanced at the clock. "Shit, Ben, it's two fucking a.m. Go to sleep."

Jake turned the light off and fell back to sleep while Ben lay on his bed plotting his next move.

"Now I'm wide awake," Ben muttered to himself. "So how the hell do you apply for a regular loan?"

He jumped out of bed, picked up his laptop, sat cross-legged on the floor in the dark, and typed '*How do I get a loan?*' into the search engine. After hitting '*enter*', he stared at the computer screen and scanned the copy. "*Shit, they check your credit rating. Those fuckers!*" Ben slammed the laptop shut, and the sound caused Jake to stir.

Ben got back into bed, stared at the ceiling, and cursed himself for the mess he had gotten himself into. Again.

Either way he figured it, he was a dead man. His father would make life a living hell and would never, ever let him live it down, making him an indentured slave or something. At least if he defaulted on his loan from Max, his agony would be over soon.

A glimmer of hope appeared as a distant memory from his economics class drifted into his consciousness. Perhaps there was another way out, one that didn't involve crossing paths with Max Marino or his father. He recalled some mumbo jumbo about managing debt and financial strategy through credit counseling, debt consolidation, and other legitimate ways to tackle financial woes, so maybe if he reached out to a credit counselor they would come up with a plan to dig himself out of this financial hole without his having to make a dangerous deal with the Devil. It wouldn't be an easy journey, and it would probably take years - and years - to pay off, and he'd never be out from under. Not ever!

"Nah, too fucking complicated," he said, and as he dug under the covers to get comfortable, he decided that selling his soul - and maybe his ass - to Max Marino was his best and fastest option.

28. A Fatuous Infatuation

ETHAN wondered why such a nice looking kid was standing alone in the corner. It was Saturday night and the Cockhound Lounge was packed and jumping. He noticed everyone but that kid was with someone. Well, except for himself, who was alone again as usual. He had a rare Saturday off, a rotation that rolled around once every eight weeks, so he made the most of it by kicking up his heels and sowing some wild oats at some other bar in the city. He tried to remember what that was called? A *busman's* something or other, he thought. Oh, who the fuck cared after three rum and cokes?

Ethan leaned across the bar and waved to the bartender. "Excuse me," he said. "Is that guy over there in the corner a regular here?"

"You could say that," the bartender said. "I think he's for rent, if you know what I mean, but you didn't hear it from me."

Ethan picked up his drink and worked his way across the room toward the kid in the corner. As he got closer, he recognized immediately why the kid had caught his eye. The short cropped blond hair, the clean-cut, handsome features, the chiseled jaw, the dreamy blue eyes, the peaches and cream complexion, the gym bod in the tight t-shirt. *Fuck me*, Ethan thought. The dude is a ringer for you-know-who.

"How's it goin'?" Ethan asked the kid.

"It's going."

"Can I buy you a drink?"

"Sure," the kid said. "I'll take a Corona."

"Comin' right up." Ethan weaved his way to the bar, a giddy excitement building in his insides. He juggled the two beers back through the nuts-to-butts crowd and was happy to see the kid hadn't bailed.

"Gracias," the kid said as Ethan handed him the cold bottle.

Ethan laughed. "Very funny."

The kid gave him a curious look. "What's funny?"

"*Corona* beer? *Gracias*?"

"I don't get it."

"Forget it." Ethan realized he was trying too hard to be jovial, and joviality was not the reason this kid was waiting in a dark corner of the Cockhound Lounge on a busy Saturday night.

The kid chugged his beer in two gulps and tossed the bottle into the blue plastic trash can he was leaning against. "So what are you looking for, man?"

Ethan's heart was pounding. "Well," he said, scanning the room nervously. "How much?"

"You can't ask me that in here, bro," the kid said. "We have to go out back." He jerked his head in the direction of a side door and Ethan followed.

As they made their way outside, Ethan couldn't believe what he was doing. He had paid for sex exactly one time before, when he was in his teens, but it was someone he knew. The kid led him around the back of the building, where they were shielded from the noise and the music of the bar.

"So, how much?" Ethan asked again, his voice shaky with anxiety.

"Depends what you're looking for," the kid said, his back against the wall, a leg propped up behind him.

"I don't know," Ethan said, feeling a bit foolish. "I've never done this before."

"Yeah, right." The kid rolled his eyes. "So, what are you into?"

Ethan shrugged and hesitated. Was this a wise decision? What if this was a setup? What if he was about to be robbed, or worse? Ethan swallowed hard and looked around. It was dark, but not so dark that people couldn't see them through the windows in the back of the bar. And it was Saturday night in a busy part of town, and Ethan was pretty sure if he called out for help someone would hear him and come running. Finally, he said, "Not sure."

The kid lifted his t-shirt to reveal a rippling washboard stomach with a light blond treasure trail leading down into his low riding jeans. Ethan looked into the kid's eyes and saw Jake Whitney, his fantasy lover, staring back, and all his reservations and intimidations vanished.

"Okay, so twenty-five bucks if all you want to do is blow me," the kid said. "Fifty, if you want me to blow you. A hundred for mutual, and if you want it up the ass, which includes a combo of all of the above, it'll cost you two hundred."

Ethan took a deep breath. "Can I ask how old you are?"

The kid sighed and pulled down the waistband on his jeans. "See the bush? Means I'm old enough."

On closer inspection Ethan decided the kid didn't look that much like Jake, although he might have passed for a reasonable facsimile in a darkened room, say, if Jake needed an understudy. But Ethan's libido had already raced past the line of demarcation and he was ready to fork over two hundred hard earned smackers for the whole enchilada.

"My apartment is only a few blocks from here," Ethan told him. "We can shower first and get comfortable."

The kid pushed off from the wall, stretched, and cracked his back. "Lead the way, dude."

Ethan walked a few paces in front, then stopped and swiveled toward the kid. "Do you have any, uh...?"

The kid tapped his pocket with his thumb. "No worries," he said.

29. The Arrangement

THE distant hum of sirens, car horns, and plane engines drowned out any rational thought that might have stopped them from taking the dangerous leap. Sitting in a U-Haul van in a dark alley near the airport, surrounded by towering buildings that blocked out the moonlight, the two guys waited for their instructions.

The reality of their situation hit Jake like a sledgehammer. They were in deep now, and there was no turning back. He exchanged a nervous glance with Ben, who struggled to stay awake.

"I can't believe you talked me into this," Jake said, his voice trembling with uncertainty.

"I didn't talk you into anything, bro," Ben replied. "This was *your* idea, okay? You said, *'I have an idea that'll get us both off the hook.'* Shit, I was ready to hit up Max Marino for a small loan, and you said that Tony was putting on the pressure for you to do a job for Max, so here we are, dude. You'll complete your obligation to Max, I'll pay off my debt so Daddy doesn't wear my nuts for cufflinks. *Badabing, badaboom,* a win-win for both of us."

Jake pulled the collar of his jacket up around his neck. "We haven't *won* anything yet," he said. "And once we're in Max's clutches, he'll keep breathing down our necks, getting us to do another job and another job and..."

"You told me Tony said we'd be in the clear."

"Tony looks out for *Tony*," Jake said, "His priority is to keep jerking Max Marino off to stay alive."

Ben rolled his eyes and released a huge sigh. "Could you, for once, focus on what's happening right now instead of imagining a dark future? This is the only way out, bro. It's a simple job. Just a drop-off. In and out. Quick cash. Lots of it. We do it, and I'm free. Excuse me, *we're* free."

Jake understood the depth of Ben's troubles, the late-night poker games, the online betting, the ominous calls from shady characters. He had always considered himself the voice of reason in their friendship, but he couldn't stand by and watch Ben get devoured by the merciless meat grinder of debt.

Jake recalled the morning he and Ben met with Tony to seal the deal. The pressure from Tony on Jake to make a delivery for Max had been escalating with each passing day.

"You know, Jake," Tony had told him, "we've been more than patient with you. It's time you started showin' some loyalty."

"Loyalty?" Jake shrugged. "I dance my ass off for you every night."

"You dance your ass off for *you*, kid, and you know it," Tony snapped. "And Max Marino provides the opportunity for you to do so. Just this once, the man asks for somethin' extra. It's not like he's askin' you to do it for nothin'. You're gettin' ten grand apiece, for cryin' out loud."

"What exactly are we transporting?" Ben asked, trying to sound confident.

"You guys are better off not knowin', okay?" Tony replied. "They need the stuff transported, and it's in your hands. What it is you're movin' don't need to matter to you. All that matters is how you boys have a unique advantage that most of us, well, don't. You're two clean-cut college kids. No one would suspect you of nothin', and that's why we need you for this here job."

Jake's concern for his safety during the upcoming deal was palpable. He looked Tony squarely in the eyes and asked, "Tony, can you guarantee our safety during this operation? What if something goes wrong?"

Tony sighed, recognizing Jake's legitimate concerns. "Look at it this way, boys, the truck won't be rented in your names, so alls you gotta do is play dumb if it comes to that. You were hired to do this here, like, whaddaya call 'em, uh, Two Hunks Haulin' Junk, or whatever the hell."

"That's true," Ben reasoned. "When you hire movers, they don't know what the hell they're moving."

Jake took a minute to consider the situation. "I don't see it quite as cut-and-dry as you guys do, but, okay, let's hear the plan."

"Here it is, so listen up." Tony leaned in closer. "A truck will already be rented at the U-Haul on Foster and State Streets. You drive there after the office is closed and park your car, then take the truck. The keys will be in it. In the glove box, you'll find a burner phone. Within a few minutes after pickin' up the truck, you'll get a text message with the address where they're gonna load up the truck. You drive there and sit on your two lazy asses till they're done loadin', then you'll get another text with the drop-off location. Same deal, you drive there, sit and wait until it's unloaded, and you drive the empty truck back to U-Haul. Easy peasy."

"Yeah," Ben said. "Sounds nice and easy and very peasy to me."

"And I'm sure I don't need to tell you, of course," Tony emphasized, "that once that load is on that truck, neither of youse two sets one single itty-bitty little *footsie toe* outside the cab of that fuckin' truck. Got that?"

Jake and Ben looked at each other, then looked back at Tony, and in unison they nodded and muttered, "Got it."

"So when do we get paid?" Ben asked.

"Max's accountant, Bruno, will drop off the cash at the bar the next day," Tony said. "I'll give it to Jake, who can count it, and then blah, blah, fuckin' blah."

Jake took a breath. "And we'll be driving across state lines?"

"Yup," Tony said. "How far across? I have no idea, but there lies the tale, gentlemen."

Jake recalled how he felt that morning, sweat forming on his brow. "And we're done after this, right? Paid in full? No more demands, no more threats?"

"Totally," Tony nodded. "Even-Steven."

"I got to pee like Seabiscuit," Ben said.

Tony pointed, "To the left behind the bar. I just put in new paper."

Ben got up and wiggled comically across the room holding his legs together. "Too much coffee, guys."

Tony jerked his chin at Jake. "I know you're doin' this to help out that bozo."

Jake pretended he didn't understand. "Bozo?"

"He must have a huge pair of stones," Tony said. "This is a pretty huge ask."

Jake drummed his fingers on the table. "Friends help friends, right, Tony?"

"You gotta ask yourself if he would do the same for you," Tony said, wagging his finger in front of Jake's face.

"Of course he would," Jake said. "I know he would."

"You sure about that?" Tony asked him. "I'm a pretty good judge of people from my bein' 'round a long time, see, and that kid don't impress me so much."

"Ben's a good guy," he told Tony. "He's a bit of a loudmouth sometimes. What can I say?"

Jake remembered how Tony looked deep into his eyes that day. "Level with me, kid," he said. "You're lettin' him keep the whole twenty grand, ain't you?"

Jake didn't answer, but he didn't have to. Tony Gaudio was no fool.

"Shit, kid, you could use that money yourself," Tony said. "You know how I know? 'Cause that asshole called Max Marino for a piddly five grand loan, and Max told him to take a hike, that's how I know."

"He did?"

"Yeah, he did."

Nope, Tony Gaudio was no fool, no fool at all.

"Earth to Jake, Earth to Jake Whitney," Ben shouted, snapping Jake back to the present. "When the hell are we gonna get that text? The truck's been loaded for almost an hour."

As if by magic, the burner phone lit up. "Finally," Jake gasped, his trembling hand picking it up to read the text message containing an address located about thirty minutes across the state line.

"It's showtime!" Ben exclaimed as Jake started up the truck and pulled out from the alley and up the ramp to the highway.

Jake's nerves were on edge, and Ben was acting like they were a pair of revelers in a college scavenger hunt. Jake impulsively checked and double-checked the GPS and the other instruments on the dashboard. Everything was in order, but he lived his life waiting for the other shoe to drop.

"Hey, bro," Ben whispered. "What do you think is in the back of this truck?"

"Don't care."

"But Benjamin is soooo curious," Ben announced. "What if it's cocaine?"

"Don't care."

"Ever tried cocaine?"

"Nope."

"Me neither."

"And if I can read your mind, Benjamin Mendelsen, and I think I can," Jake said, "lemme tell you right now that you aren't going to."

When all else failed, Ben pulled out the cutes. "But Benjamin is soooo curious."

"Too fuckin' bad."

As they drove down the highway, Jake tried to calm his racing thoughts by focusing on his cover story. He was a college student, that's all, hired by an anonymous party to deliver a load to a warehouse. He had no idea what was in the truck, and he certainly wasn't involved with the mob.

But as he passed a police car on the shoulder, he couldn't help but feel as if the officers were staring right at him. His heart pounded as he waited for them to start chasing him, but they didn't budge. Maybe Ben was right. Maybe he was always time-warping into dark visions of the future.

"Dude, I have to pee like Man O' War," Ben said.

"Are you kidding me?" Jake said. "You always have to pee like a racehorse, but apparently you have a bladder like My Little Pony."

"Stop up here, dude," Ben said, tapping his knuckle on the window. "I'll whip it out and be finished in a flash."

As Jake waited for Ben to complete his mission, he heard the clanging of metal scraping against metal as the rear door on the truck lifted, and the blood coursing through his veins turned to ice water. He couldn't believe his ears. "*I. Am. Going. To. Kill. That. Motherfucker,*" he mumbled under his breath. Then he heard the door drop and the latch engage, and Ben rejoined him in the cab wearing a cat-that-ate-the-cream grin on his face.

Ben clapped his hands and rubbed them together. "Let's go, bro. Onward and upward."

"Feel better, *Fluttershy*, after your ginormous piss?" Jake said. "Okay, where'd you put it?"

Ben shrugged. "It's in my pocket."

Jake rested his pounding skull on the back of the seat and closed his eyes. "Jesus Christ," he sighed.

"Dude, when are we *ever* gonna get a blow of totally free coke?" Ben jabbered. "And no worries, either. One of the bags had the tiniest rip. They'll blame the dudes at the warehouse."

"You are a *moron*," Jake said. "Now if we get stopped, we can't claim innocence."

"We're not getting stopped, Mr. Disaster."

"What if there's a... a *gizmo* in the truck that tells them we got out of the cab?" Jake surmised.

"What *if*? What *if*?" Ben mocked. "What if *aliens* attack us, and they take us to Planet Butt Cheeks, and they force us to perform rim jobs on the King of the Ass Munchers?"

As they approached the drop-off point, Jake couldn't help but feel like they were driving into a trap. The location was an abandoned warehouse at the edge of town. Its windows were shattered, and the place reeked of decay. As soon as they pulled in front of the warehouse, they were met by a team who unloaded the truck in record time and sent them and the empty truck back on their way. Ben and Jake could practically hear each other's hearts pounding in their chests.

"Twenty-thousand *motherfucking* dollars!" Ben cheered. "You know what? That was so damn *easy* and so freakin' *peasy,* I would gladly be down for another of these fuckin' heists, man. Seriously, it felt like we were in a fuckin' action movie!"

Jake looked at Ben as if he were hearing things. "You'll be doing it alone, lunatic."

"What're you talking about?"

"Better start looking for a new roommate," Jake said. "I have enough saved to get my own place."

"You serious, bro?"

"As a fuckin' heart attack, *bro.*"

30. A Funny Thing Happened on the Way to the Strip Club

THE life of a comedian brings its own special challenges. It is a common opinion that all clowns secretly desire to play Hamlet. Not so with Leo Shaw, who just wanted to make 'em laugh. But he faced tough crowds, hecklers, and the constant need to innovate and refine his material. He embraced it all, though, using his experiences and observations from his day job at the dollar store, and his night gig dancing in the buff, as a wellspring of inspiration.

One evening at an open mic, Leo was informed that a talent scout from a prominent comedy club happened to be in the audience. With sweaty palms and trembling knees, Leo stepped up to the microphone and delivered a set that was, by *his* standards, impeccable, and afterward would receive a review that would challenge that opinion.

"Ladies and gentlemen," the club's M.C. announced, "The Belly Laugh Comedy Club is proud to present, in his first time on our stage, a bright new comic, so put your hands together for Mr. Leo Shaw!"

Polite applause.

"Thank you, thank you. Wow, what a great crowd tonight. You make me feel like an adult. And you know you're an adult when you get excited about buying a new kitchen appliance. I mean, I practically threw a party when I got a toaster. My friends were like, 'Leo, it's just a toaster,' and I said, 'No, it's a magic *crisper*!'"

Coughs.

"You know, I used to work at a dollar store, and let me tell you, people get really picky about what they're willing to spend just one dollar on. I had a lady once ask me if she could negotiate the price of a sponge. I said, 'Lady, it's a sponge, not a *used car*!'"

Moans.

"I recently turned twenty-six, yes, twenty-freaking-six, and I realized my metabolism is like a sloth on vacation. I gained three pounds just by looking at a pizza. It's like my body is saying, 'You want to eat that? Prepare for a *lifetime commitment!*'"

Yawns.

"I tried to impress a date by taking her to an art museum, but I don't know anything about art. So, I just stood in front of a random painting and said, 'This one's a masterpiece. It really speaks to my soul.' She replied, 'Leo, that's the *exit sign!*'"

Sniffs.

"I love watching cooking shows, don't you?"

No response.

"But they always make it seem so easy. They're like, 'Just sauté the onions and flambé the sauce.' Meanwhile, I'm in my kitchen and my smoke alarm's going off like, 'Call the *fire department!*'"

Groans.

"I used to be an exotic dancer, and let me tell you, it's a unique job. My friends would ask me what I did for a living, and I'd say, 'I'm a professional twirler.' They'd look at me like, 'Baton or hula hoop?' I said, 'My *penis!*'"

Walkouts.

"People often assume exotic dancers have glamorous lives. But, folks, let me set the record straight. I once danced for a bachelorette party in a room that looked like it had been hit by a glitter tornado. I'm still finding glitter *where the moon don't shine!*"

Sneeze. (The sneeze got a laugh)

"People think exotic dancers are the life of the party, but behind the scenes, it's all about pain and suffering. I once glued a thong to my crotch so it would stay in place. Talk about wardrobe malfunction, when I took it off, it was more like a *body wax!*"

Sighs.

"Now, you know what's the best thing about being an exotic dancer? The outfits, of course! I mean, who doesn't love a good *thong*, am I right? Ever wear one? It's like a permanent *wedgie!*"

A glass dropped. (The dropped glass got applause)

"I've even had some patrons try to tip me with their last dollar, literally their *last* dollar bill. I lost my dignity and they lost their *savings account!*"

Snores.

"I've learned that exotic dancing is all about confidence. It's like a confidence boot camp. I'd walk out on stage thinking, 'I got this,' and then I'd jump a foot in the air when some grandma shoves a dollar bill between my butt cheeks. So the score was confidence, one, Leo, *zero!*"

Someone shouted, "Zero is right."

"Well, thank you folks for putting up with me. You've been a great audience," but no one heard him because they were all talking amongst themselves by then.

Leo strolled to the bar in need of something to wet his parched whistle. "Is the talent scout still here?" he asked the bartender.

The bartender replied, "Yes, he's hanging from the overhead light in the men's room."

31. Deeper Into Sarah

"I STILL can't believe you called me," Jake said, gazing at Sarah's beautiful face as they walked through the dingy hallway of his apartment building.

"Sorry I had to call the bar," she said. "I had no other way to reach you."

He flashed a goofy smile. "You could have asked Brett."

"You're a laugh riot!" A sudden thought caused her to panic. "Tony won't tell him, will he?"

"You didn't tell him who you were, did you?"

Sarah shook her head. "I just gave him the number to give to you."

They stopped in front of room number twelve, and Jake took out his keys. "I have to warn you," he said as he put the key in the door. "It's small, but it's clean."

Sarah's eyes widened. "What is?"

"My apartment, of course," he said, pushing the door open. "Excuse the clutter."

Sarah giggled. "You said it was clean."

"It's *clean* clutter," he said. "Work and school don't leave much time for housekeeping."

"As long as the sheets are clean, who cares?" she said, her voice low and breathy.

The apartment was small and cramped, and so dimly lit she could barely make out the outlines of the furniture.

He tossed his keys onto a small table. "Let's get some light in here," he said, switching on a lamp. "Make yourself comfortable while I grab us some drinks."

Sarah nodded and made her way over to the couch, sinking into its worn and overstuffed cushions. She glanced around at the cluttered room, taking in the stacks of papers and books scattered across the coffee table. There was a faint smell of old pizza hanging in the air.

Jake emerged from the kitchen with two beers in hand, the cool glass bottles sweating in the heat. "Cheers," he said, clinking his bottle against hers.

Sarah took a sip, the cold liquid running down her throat and soothing her parched mouth. Jake settled onto the couch next to her. He kicked off his sneakers, and their thighs touched. They sat in silence for a few minutes, sipping their beers and listening to the summer sounds of the city outside, the distant roar of traffic, and the occasional honking horn.

Jake put down his beer and placed his hand on her knee. She could feel the warmth of his palm through the fabric of her jeans. "I've been thinking about you all day," he said. "I kept checking and rechecking the paper with your number on it, amazed at my good luck."

Sarah felt her heart quicken and turned to face him, their eyes inches apart. "I've been thinking about you too," she whispered.

Jake leaned in and captured her mouth with his, pushing past her lips with his tongue. Her aroma was invigorating, not a specific scent, but something fresh, pure, and new. He felt like a kid kissing a girl for the first time. Granted, he hadn't kissed as many as Ben Mendelsen claimed he had, although he suspected a few of the notches on Ben's belt to be an exaggeration and probably self-inflicted.

Sarah moaned into the kiss, her fingers combing through Jake's hair as his hand moved higher up her leg. She gasped in response to the friction of his fingers and felt the heat rising inside of her.

Jake pulled away from the kiss, his eyes heavy with desire. "I want you," he said, his voice husky.

They rose from the couch and stumbled their way toward the bed. He quickly stripped off his clothes, then pushed her onto the bed, unzipped her jeans and pulled them off. She pulled him on top of her and guided him with her hand.

"I've never felt anything like this before," he murmured as she squirmed under him with pleasure. She rocked her hips to meet his and ran her hands over the smooth planes of his back to feel the muscles flex beneath her fingers.

"Harder," she begged, and moved her hands down to his taut buttocks, digging her nails in to spur him on. When his back arched, her body shuddered.

They lay there, still gripping each other, afraid to let go, understanding what they had shared was more than merely physical, and neither one of them remembered falling asleep.

32. Brutal

THE air in The Velvet Joystick was thick with tension as the lights overhead cast an eerie glow on the faces of Jake, Brett, Leo, and Ethan, who were huddled at a corner table. Their expressions were etched with disbelief and sorrow.

The door swung open, and a hushed silence descended upon the room. Detective Curtis Pismo entered with two police officers, his solemn expression signaling the gravity of the situation. He made his way over to the group of friends, casting a sympathetic glance their way.

"Is it true?" Brett asked.

"I'm afraid so," the detective replied. "We have a positive I.D."

"What the hell happened?" Leo inquired.

Pismo pushed his hat off his forehead and sighed. "It has all the earmarks of a mob hit."

Tony appeared from the back room and joined the group around the table. "It's him, isn't it?" he asked.

"Yes, sir," Pismo confirmed. "It's definitely Marco Santangelo's body, and it's not a pretty sight. He was brutally mutilated."

"A mob hit, Tony," Ethan added.

Tony slumped into a chair. "Marco was more than an employee. He was like a son to me," he said. "Where was he found?"

"The waterfront," Pismo said. "Near the end of Pier 27."

The news hit like a sledgehammer, and the friends exchanged looks of despair and anger. Leo clenched his fists, while Jake lowered his head, struggling to hold back tears. Ethan, the most impulsive of the group, muttered something under his breath, barely audible.

Brett, the most level-headed among them, turned to Detective Pismo. "You'll find who did this, right? Marco didn't deserve this."

The detective nodded, his expression pained. "We'll do our best, but you all need to stay safe. Be careful who you associate with. Somebody is playing a dangerous game."

"Is there anything we can do, detective?" Jake asked.

"I'll be back in a day or two to ask a few questions," he said, scattering some business cards on the table. "Here's my number if you need it. In the meantime, put on your thinking caps and see if you can come up with anyone who might have a clue about who did this, or if something happened to raise a red flag. Anything you can come up with will help, no matter how insignificant you might think it is."

"No prob, detective," Tony assured.

Detective Pismo said goodnight and left with the two police officers following behind.

"What the fuck?" Brett said.

Leo shook his head. "I just saw Marco two nights ago."

Jake put his head down on the table. "I saw him *last* night. We left together, and I walked him to the bus."

"He seem okay to you?" Tony asked.

Jake sighed. "Yeah, fine."

Tony scanned the faces around the table. "Anybody have anything?"

The group looked at each other expectantly, then sat in somber silence, each lost to their own thoughts. The only sound in the room was the soft buzzing of the neon lights and the whirring of the ceiling fans.

"Listen, boys," Tony said, his voice heavy with emotion. "I know we're all feelin' angry and lost right now, but we need to keep our heads cool. Let's not make any reckless decisions. Be careful what we say to the cops, okay?"

"He's right," Brett said, nodding his head. "We need to be smart about this. We don't want anything to interfere with what we do here at the club."

Ethan stood up, knocking over his chair. "Fuck that, Brett," he said, his voice rising. "Max Marino is at the bottom of this, I can feel it in my balls."

"You feel a lot of things down there," Brett said.

The rest of the group looked at Ethan, surprised by his outburst. Tony raised an eyebrow and leaned forward. "What makes you say somethin' like that, Ethan?"

Ethan paced around the table, his hands balled into fists. "Everybody knows Marco was involved with Veronica Marino. What else do you need to know? If it quacks like a duck..."

"Easy, Ethan." Tony raised his hand. "We don't know nothin' for certain yet."

"I do," Ethan said. "I saw them together at the Cockhound one night."

"Ain't that a gay bar?" Tony asked.

"Well, that makes sense," Brett said. "Ethan is gayer than a Christmas sweater."

Ethan looked at Brett with hatred in his eyes. "Fuck you, Brett."

"I know you'd like to," Brett said, "but I'm taken, dude. Oh, yeah, and I'm straight."

"Why the heck would Marco take Mrs. Marino to a gay bar, anyway?" Leo asked.

"Less of a chance they'd be seen together," Ethan said. "We can't let Marino get away with this."

Tony shook his head. "You're jumpin' to conclusions, Ethan. There's no proof for what you're sayin', and if you want to mess with Max Marino, you'll bring The Velvet Joystick and yourself down with it. You'll start a war, you hear me? Max Marino sees us all as small potatoes, and he'll crush us like bugs."

Jake looked up, his eyes clouded with fear. "What exactly are you suggesting we do, Ethan?"

"We bring Max and his evil empire down, blow the whistle on him." Ethan's voice was low and dangerous.

"Come on, Ethan," Brett said. "I'm sure you've got better things to blow."

"Alright, guys," Tony said. "Enough already! Youse're all actin' like a bunch of high school kids. Let's chill out and see what the cops come back with."

The door to the club burst open, and the imposing figure of Max Marino, accompanied by his two faithful goons, stepped inside. The group turned to look, their mouths agape. Marino's eyes scanned the room, taking in the tense atmosphere, before landing on Tony.

"What the heck is goin' on here, Tony?" Max said, his voice heavy and menacing. "Why are there cops outside?"

Tony took a deep breath. "There's been a situation, Max. Marco's dead."

Max's face contorted in confusion. "Who the fuck is Marco?"

"One of our dancers," Tony said.

"One of them strippers, ya mean?" Max asked. "So who done it?"

"That's what the police are tryin' to figure out," Tony said.

"They killed him in *here?*" Max asked. "In the club?"

"No, his body was found on Pier 27," Tony explained.

"Tough luck," Max said. "They find a lot of faggots out there. You know, from pickin' up rough trade by the waterfront that don't turn out so good?"

Tony glanced over at Ethan and could see violent hate in his eyes. He braced himself and said a quiet prayer that the boy would keep his mouth shut and Max Marino wouldn't bring the whole place down like Sodom and Gomorrah.

"Can I offer you somethin', Max?" Tony said.

"Like what?" Max grumped.

"I don't know," Tony shrugged. "A drink, somethin' to eat, maybe?"

"I own everything in this joint, Tony," Max said. "And I don't need you to get it for me." He gestured to his goons and snapped his fingers. "Let's get out of here. Keep me posted on this, Tony."

Max Marino stomped out of The Velvet Joystick like visiting royalty, followed by his two fawning servants. Tony breathed a sigh of relief, and the boys exchanged uneasy glances. The tension in the room was oppressive.

"I think I need a change of underwear," Leo said, and he actually got a laugh.

33. The Lady or the Tiger?

JAKE felt like a pressure cooker about to blow. The brutal demise of Marco Santangelo threw the fear of God, and also the fear of Max Marino, into him. He had been harboring his secret affair for weeks, and it was gnawing at his soul and threatening to consume him. The weight of it bore down on him, and he couldn't keep it hidden any longer.

"Well," Ben remarked as he entered the apartment, scanning the disarray, "It's nice to see that you have done absolutely *nothing* to fix the place up. You moved out of the dorm and left me paying double for this?"

"It's worth it not to hear you snore," Jake retorted. "Want a beer?"

"Does the pope shit in the woods?" Ben plopped down on the couch and tossed a copy of the racing form on the coffee table. "So how would you classify your choice of decor? Early *who farted*?"

Jake strolled in from the kitchen, two beer bottles in hand, and tossed one to Ben. "Given the time I spend here, juggling school during the day and the bar at night, I could save money on rent by sleeping at the bus station."

Ben's gaze wandered to the unkempt bed. "Looks like the mattress has seen some action," he noted, taking a sip from his bottle. "Are you aware that fitted sheets are supposed to *fit* over all four corners?"

Jake leaned back, rubbing the cool bottle against his forehead. "I promise I'll tidy up before the House and Garden photographer gets here."

Ben arched an eyebrow. "Who's the lucky lady?"

"What are you talking about?"

"Puh-leeze, dude," Ben chuckled. "I smell sex in here."

"Ben," Jake began, his voice barely above a whisper, "I need somebody to talk to."

"What's eatin' you, bro?" Ben asked. "I hope, whatever it is, she's *hot.*"

Jake took a deep breath, then downed his beer, as if mustering courage. "You heard what happened to Marco, right?"

"Yeah," Ben replied. "The stripper who got himself bumped off?"

"I'm worried the same thing is gonna happen to me."

"They're saying it was a mob hit," Ben said. "What do you have to do with the mob?"

Jake braced himself, preparing to unveil the big reveal. "Marco was screwing Max Marino's wife."

"Way to go, Marco," Ben said. "So what's that got to do with you?"

Jake hesitated. "I'm sleeping with her too."

Ben swallowed hard. "Holy shit."

Jake placed the empty bottle on the coffee table, his hands trembling. "I couldn't resist her, Ben. It was like getting sucked into the eye of a tornado."

"I hear ya, dude," Ben nodded. "Pussy'll do that to you every time. So how old is this bitch?"

"I dunno," he shrugged. "Fifty, maybe."

"Fifty?"

"Ben, I'm terrified Marino will find out and I'll end up like Marco."

Ben leaned back and put his feet on the coffee table. He had his own worries, his own fears, his own addictions, but at this moment, Jake's headache trumped his. Getting intimately involved with the wife of a mob boss, especially one with a reputation as ruthless as Max Marino's, could be a one-way ticket to Armageddon.

"You gotta give that mafia cunt the heave-ho," Ben affirmed. "That's all there is to it."

Jake shook his head. "Not that easy."

"Why not?"

"It's like 'The Lady or the Tiger?'"

"It's like huh?"

"That famous short story," Jake said.

"Dude," Ben said, "you know I don't read."

"A Roman gladiator is ordered to pick one of two doors, okay?" Jake explained. "Behind door *one* is a slave girl who's gonna fuck his brains out, and behind door *two* there's a tiger ready to tear him to pieces."

"Well," Ben said, "that's a no-brainer."

"Ah, yes, but here's the catch," Jake continued. "The gladiator has a girlfriend, see, and she finds out which door is which, and she's gonna give him a heads up."

"I see where you're going with this," Ben said. "Whichever door the twat tells the dude to go for, she loses him. Better he should be cat food, right?"

"And that, my friend, is my situation." Jake sighed and slumped in frustration. "If I keep seeing Veronica, Max will kill me. If I break it off with Veronica, she has the power to set me up."

Ben pondered for a moment, then burst into laughter. "I think this is what's called being caught between a rock and a *hard-on*."

"You should write material for Leo Shaw," Jake said. "I need to think through this Veronica situation."

"But you can't live in constant fear either, dude," Ben advised. "That's no way to live."

Jake took a deep breath and exhaled. "I wish I could approach life as carefree as you do."

A mischievous glint filled Ben's eyes as he stood up and pulled a plastic sandwich bag filled with white powder from his jeans' pocket. "Look what little Benji brung along."

"Oh, shit," Jake gasped. "I'm amazed you haven't snorted it all yet."

"It really belongs to both of us, dude," Ben said. "I mean, you did all the driving and I made out like a bandit, pun totally intended. And, by the way, the other shoe never dropped, did it?"

"What other shoe?"

"Nobody said anything about the missing blow, did they?"

"Well, no," Jake shook his head. "Not yet, anyway."

"Fuck, dude, that ship has sailed," Ben laughed. "I think we're in the clear. See, didn't I tell you, Mr. Disaster?"

"I have enough problems, asshole. The coke is all yours," Jake said, reclining on the couch and releasing a sigh with the force of a Category 4 hurricane. "I'll stick to beer, if that's okay with you?"

"No skin off my pork whistle," Ben said as he pulled out a plastic straw.

34. Living It Up

BEN Mendelsen felt on top of the world after Jake took his hand and pulled him out of the hole he had dug for himself. The twenty thousand bucks in cold, hard cash were still sitting in a cookie tin, stashed in a pillowcase, and buried under a pile of dirty laundry in his dorm room, where he now lived alone.

He had made a promise to himself that he would never again venture down the primrose path of excess and debauchery. His primary concern now was to focus on improving his grades, which had suffered considerably during his chaotic period. He reasoned that a young man needed to sow his wild oats when he's young, and, well, while he still had some oats left to sow.

His promise to be a good boy was, alas, one more risky bet, a different kind of bet, but a gamble nonetheless. Ben's first inclination was to invest the money before repaying his debts, to see if he might possibly siphon off some profit while he still had that much cash in his hot little hands. And think how proud daddy would be.

"But fuck that," he thought. "What makes turning your hard-earned cash over to some broker you've never laid eyes on any different than standing at a roulette table waiting for the little white ball to land on a number that will make your dreams come true? It's instant gratification, an orgasm without the bother of having to talk to anybody afterward, and, shit, the payoffs are way better.

So, these were the thoughts running through Ben's mind as he sat in front of a quarter slot machine on a gambling boat anchored not ten feet from shore, surrounded by nicotine-addicted senior citizens tethered to their Visa cards by alligator clips as they maxed themselves out.

Ben tunneled under his dirty socks and underwear to retrieve the pillowcase and pop open that cookie tin to peel away a few hundred, okay, a few thousand, bucks, and chalk it up to an evening's entertainment. Life is, after all, very short, and you are a *very* long time dead.

But the spinning images of cherries, lemons, oranges, and bananas weren't cutting it for him. (*And what's with all the fruit?*) "Damn," he mumbled under his breath. "Twenty thousand bucks is eighty thousand quarters. Sitting at a slot machine waiting for it to poop out a few measly coins is a freakin' lifetime sentence. Imagine what the interest on my debts would be by then? I'll be older than these other rotting zombies when I'm done, with one foot in the grave and the other on a banana peel." (*Again, what's with all the fruit?*) A slot machine was as satisfying to Ben as a can of near-beer would have been to a die-hard alcoholic.

Long story short, it didn't take long before Ben moved to the blackjack table, doubling down on each hand and ignoring the disapproving glances of the dealer. He was sure he could win it all back, like he had many times before. And if that didn't work, there was always the craps table, the roulette wheel, or the sports betting room. Life was full of opportunities, and all a guy had to do was roll up his sleeves and dig in.

As the night wore on, despite mounting bad luck, Ben felt he was only getting started. He knew he should stop, cut his losses, and walk away while he still had some of his stash left, but the allure of the game was too strong, and the prospect of salvation through the next shuffle, the next roll, the next spin, was too promising to ignore.

Ben ordered another drink from the scantily clad cocktail waitress who had been flirting with him all night. He downed it in one gulp before signaling for another to calm his nerves, clear his head, and come up with a strategy. There had to be a way to turn his luck around, to win it all back and come out on top.

That's when he spotted the stunning redhead at the far end of the craps table, her eyes fixed on him with a predatory gleam. She was beautiful, with full lips painted a deep shade suggesting they had experienced intense combat. The lady was winning big, accumulating credits with every roll of the dice. Ben thought he could use her good fortune to his advantage. Maybe she was lonely, and it had been some time since she had wrapped her legs around a college boy. He wasn't too proud to accept a donation for his masculine services when the chips were down.

He walked over and introduced himself, flashing his most charming smile. "Hey there, I couldn't help but notice you're on a winning streak," he said. "Mind if I watch?"

"You like to watch?" she purred, running her tongue around her lips. She sized him up, and Ben could feel her laser-like eyes burning through him. He knew she wasn't his usual type. She was older, more sophisticated than the college girls he was used to, but he was confident he could charm her. And maybe, just maybe, she'd be willing to share her good fortune with him.

"Yeah, I like to watch," he replied, leaning against the table and trying to look casual. "Especially when someone's on a hot streak like you are."

She chuckled, her eyes dancing with amusement. "You're not hard to look at," she said. "What's your name?"

"Ben," he offered his hand, which she took in a firm grip.

"Maggie," she replied, still holding his hand. "And I think you're just the distraction I need tonight, honey."

Ben felt a surge of excitement. This was his chance to turn his luck around. He moved closer to her, feeling the warmth of her body. He could smell her perfume, a heady mix of musk and flowers, and his pulse quickened.

He watched her expertly toss the dice, her nimble fingers skillfully caressing them. "You're a natural at this," he said.

Maggie's eyes never left his as she placed a bet and rolled again, landing on a winning combination. Ben's heart raced, and he knew he had to act quickly to maintain her attention.

"Hey, how about we make a little bet?" he suggested, leaning closer. "I bet I can guess the next roll, and if I'm right, you give me half of your winnings."

Maggie raised an eyebrow, a wry smile on her lips. "You're a bold one, aren't you?" she said, her interest evident in her eyes. "All right, I'll take that bet. What's your guess?"

Ben studied the dice for a moment, then looked up at Maggie. "Seven," he said with confidence.

Maggie rolled the dice, and Ben held his breath as the cubes bounced across the table. When they came to rest, he spotted three dots on one and four on the other.

"Yes!" he exclaimed, pumping his fist in the air.

Maggie chuckled, shaking her head. "You got lucky, handsome," she said. "But, sure, I'll keep my end of the bargain."

She reached into her purse, counted out half of her winnings, and handed it to him.

"Thanks," he said, feeling a rush of excitement. "This could be the start of something big."

"Your turn," she said, a mischievous glint in her eye. "If I win this one, I get all my money back. If I lose, you owe me a drink."

"That's more than fair," Ben agreed.

Maggie's luck took a turn for the worse as she rolled snake eyes. Ben could see the frustration on her face, but she masked it with a nonchalant comment, "Don't worry about it. It's just a game."

"So, where would you like to have your drink?" he asked.

"In my room, of course," she replied, as she snapped her purse closed with a flourish and swept towards the elevator, Ben following like a dutiful puppy.

It didn't take long for Ben to figure out that Maggie was more than just a skilled gambler. She was a master of seduction. Before he knew it, they were both undressed, her lips exploring his chest, and her tongue toying with a nipple. Her mouth moved lower, her lips and tongue caressing every inch.

"You're a natural at this too," he whispered, recalling his earlier observation about those lips. Maggie was unlike any woman he'd been with before, older, more experienced, and she knew exactly what she wanted. Her nimble fingers guided him toward the warm, wet center of her body, and she let out a moan of pleasure as he began to thrust with passion.

As the bed creaked with each sensual movement, Ben wasn't sure how long he could maintain the frantic pace. He also had a nagging feeling in the pit of his stomach that he was no longer in control of the situation.

A loud knock at the door, followed by a booming male voice shouted, "Open up, Cecilia!"

"Hold on," Maggie muttered, her hand brushing Ben's shrinking tumescence as she dismounted.

Ben heard the door open with a flurry of whispers and mutterings, and scrambled into his pants. He heard Maggie say, "What the hell took you so long?" and the male voice answered, "I gave you a fucking hour." Then Maggie said, "That's too long."

Ben was searching for a missing sock when Maggie and the guy entered the bedroom. The guy was holding a gun. "Where's the money, kid?" he said.

"Probably in his pants," Maggie said.

"Don't move, kid," the guy said, as Maggie, or Cecilia, patted him down. She found the rest of Ben's stash in his left pant pocket, a good seven or eight thousand dollars, and tossed it toward the guy with the gun.

"*Your* cash is in the *other* pocket," Ben said. "Why not take it all?"

"It's counterfeit, kid," the guy replied. "Think we were born yesterday? Are my shoes labeled 'left' and 'right'?"

"Finish getting dressed and get the fuck out," Maggie, or Cecilia, said. Whoever she was, her body was as pale white and naked as the day she was born, except, of course, for the red bush.

35. He Shoots, He Scores

"WELL, hey," Jake exclaimed, startled, as he stood in his apartment doorway wearing pajama bottoms and holding a Diet Coke. In the background, a basketball game blared from the television. "What are you doing here?"

"That's the kind of greeting a girl likes to hear," Sarah responded. "Who's playing?"

"Huh?"

"The game you're watching," she clarified. "Who's playing?"

Jake continued to stare. "Uh, the Knicks and, uh, some other team."

"Who cares?" she interrupted. "I've decided to move in with you." She held a small overnight bag.

Jake hesitated, leaning in as if he hadn't heard her correctly. "Excuse me?"

"Why don't you invite me in?" she suggested. "I feel like a Jehovah's Witness standing here."

"They travel in pairs."

"Do you mind?" she huffed, squeezing by.

"I'm not sure." He stepped aside and closed the door behind them, his startled expression still in place and his heart pounding. He'd forgotten how beautiful she was.

"Sorry for the last-minute shock," she said, "but I figured if I just showed up, you couldn't throw me out. It's easier to ask forgiveness than permission."

"Then this is not a joke?" he said, still standing by the door, barefoot and shirtless. "You are serious about...?"

"Serious as a heart attack," she confirmed, "one of which you appear to have had."

"Move in with me? But why?"

"Well, I've given it lots of serious consideration," she explained, "and this place is so much more elegant than my humble apartment."

"It is?"

"No."

Jake put the soda can down and rubbed his hands together. "I, uh, I don't know what to say. This is kind of sudden."

"Spontaneity keeps the heart young, or so they say," she noted. "Amy got married and moved out, so I thought it was a perfect opportunity to start fresh. And also a good way to avoid paying the entire rent myself."

"Using me as a convenience, eh? Look, we've only gone out a few times," he said. "Are you sure about this?"

"Gone *out*?" She gestured toward the bed. "You call the acrobatics that took place over there 'going out'? I'm happy to see we didn't bust it."

Jake put his hands on his hips, then crossed his arms, and finally dropped them by his side, obviously not knowing what to do with them. "Going out, staying in, whatever."

Sarah held up the overnight bag. "I brought a few things."

"Wow," he said. "Where will we put it all?"

"We can get my other stuff tomorrow," she said, her eyes scanning the apartment.

"Sarah, before we get carried away..."

"What incredibly dumb thing are you about to say?" Sarah was still checking out the apartment.

"Hello!" Jake cleared his throat. "There's an elephant in the room here."

"Well, that's gotta go," she said. "Those things eat a *ton*. I'm thinking maybe a nice occasional table instead."

"An occasional table?" he said. "What is it the rest of the time?"

Sarah rolled her eyes. "Such a funny man."

"The elephant I was referring to," he said, "is named Brett Booth."

"What a funny name for an elephant," she said. "I prefer Dumbo, don't you, or Jumbo, or Gumbo?"

Jake's frustration was mounting. "How about dropping the kooky rom-com cutie pie act and tell me what's going on."

"Full disclosure, okay?" she said. "Your genitalia is way prettier than his. Is that enough of a reason? His balls are saggy, and yours are nice and tight."

"Okay, that's good enough," he said, and he lunged across the room, wrapped his arms around her, and kissed her deeply, leaving her breathless. "I missed you so much," he whispered in her ear.

"I thought maybe your feet were glued to the floor over there," she said with a chuckle. "And could you maybe lower the TV, please? Your neighbors must love you."

"Damn, the score's ten-nothing," he said, lowering the volume slightly.

"I can barely hear myself think," she said. "That's one habit you'll need to break. I like quiet."

"So do Brett's balls really sag that much?" he asked. "I'm gonna have to razz him about it."

"You are not!" Sarah punched his arm in jest. "Brett was driving me crazy, to tell you the honest truth. It's why I never moved in with him. He kept begging and pleading. I mean, Amy was no picnic either, but I didn't have to sleep with her."

"Well, they say two can live as cheap as one," he said.

"That's why I'm moving in," she told him. "But, Jake, we need to talk."

He looked at her and sighed. "That line usually comes much later in a relationship."

"No, this is important," she said with great gravity.

Jake appeared ashen, the color draining out of his face like the mercury in a cold thermometer. "Oh, shit."

"Down, boy. Relax," she said. "No, I'm not pregnant."

He gripped his chest and flopped on the couch. "Thank you, Jesus."

Sarah took a deep breath. "This place is getting a makeover."

Jake blinked. "Why?"

"Why?" She threw her arms up and spun around. "Because you deserve a more vibrant and inviting space, that's why. Hell, *we* deserve a more vibrant and inviting space."

Jake was a bit apprehensive, realizing his apartment was far from a designer's dream. "You sure about this? It's quite a project."

"Absolutely sure," Sarah nodded. "There is nothing an artist loves more than the challenge of a blank canvas."

"My budget is about as tight as, well, my *balls*," he said. "For lack of a better comparison."

"No worries," she told him. "My job gives me access to amazing resources. We can get everything we need on loan from my office. It won't cost us a thing."

Jake's apprehension faded and he detected genuine excitement in Sarah's eyes. "I'd be a fool to argue with that."

Sarah walked around the apartment, pointing out what could stay and what needed to go. "We'll get rid of that old couch and coffee table. We can replace them with something more modern and comfortable. Your TV stand also needs an update. I'll bring in a sleeker, more functional one, in a darker wood, perhaps."

Jake listened, feeling a mix of nervousness and anticipation. "And I'll bet you'll want to put up curtains."

"Hell, yes!" Sarah smiled. "I can't believe you walk around in the *buff* without curtains on the windows."

Jake gestured to himself with both thumbs. "Stripper!"

"Yes, definitely new curtains," she said. "Something to let in more natural light. I'll add some colorful accents with throw pillows and wall art. It's all going to make a world of difference in here."

Jake couldn't help but smile at her infectious enthusiasm. "I trust your judgment completely."

Sarah hugged him tightly. "You won't regret this, Jake. We're going to make this place feel like a real home."

"I'm glad you're here," he said.

And they kissed passionately as the announcer on the TV exclaimed, *"He shoots! He scores!"*

36. Spinning the Plates

JAKE Whitney sat at a corner table in the college cafeteria trying to remain inconspicuous. Word had spread across campus that anyone interested could see him in the altogether three times nightly at The Velvet Joystick. He didn't care who showed up to watch, but he was growing weary of the obnoxious comments he had to endure during the day when fully clothed.

Nervously tapping his fingers on the worn wooden surface, he checked his watch, awaiting the arrival of Ben Mendelsen. Jake needed someone to confide in, and Ben was the only one who knew where the skeletons were buried in his past. He was also concerned about Ben's current state. Since Jake had moved out of the dorm, Ben no longer had him around to serve as his Jiminy Cricket.

Just as Jake was about to send him a terse "Where the fuck are you?" text message, Ben stumbled into the cafeteria, engrossed in a video on his phone, his disheveled appearance revealing a night of debauchery. They exchanged a half-hearted hug before taking their seats.

Ben thrust his phone, with the video playing, in front of Jake's face. "Have you seen this crazy guy?" He was referring to a YouTube video from the old Ed Sullivan Show in which a man kept ten dinner plates spinning on top of ten sticks.

"That's my life right there," Jake said.

"I've never seen that before," Ben said, collapsing into a chair. "Gotta love YouTube, right?"

"You look like boiled crap," Jake said, trying to hide his concern.

"I love you, too," Ben replied, running a hand through his mussy hair. "I guess you could say I've hit a rough patch."

"Rough patch? You look like you've been through a *tsunami*." Jake prodded further. "What's going on?"

Ben hesitated, then finally admitted, "I flushed the whole twenty grand down the shitter, man."

Jake winced. "I knew you should have let me be your banker until you were ready to settle up. You gambled the whole stash?"

Ben took a deep breath and exhaled. "Not exactly," he said. "I blew, like, half of it, and this bitch rolled me for the rest."

"Let me guess," Jake said. "You met her at the roulette table."

Ben shook his head. "Craps."

"And you went to her room, of course," Jake continued. "And while she was riding the baloney pony, her boyfriend relieved you of your net worth."

"Damn," Ben said. "Were you under the bed?"

"No," Jake said, "I've seen that movie a million times. I hope the sex was worth it."

Ben rolled his eyes. "I didn't even bust."

Jake didn't want to judge Ben, considering the tangled mess his own life had become. He opened up to his old friend. "Listen, I've got my own problems, too. I'm juggling school, the job at the bar, and two women."

"*Two* women?" Ben raised an eyebrow. "Poor, poor you."

"Thanks," Jake said. "I can feel the sympathy radiating off your body."

"Is the Mafia princess still busting your stones?" Ben asked.

"Oh, and Sarah moved in with me."

"With you?" Ben exclaimed. "In that shithole?"

"It's her blank canvas," Jake clarified.

"Huh?"

"She's giving my crib a makeover," Jake explained. "She's an interior decorator, you know?"

"That shit's not cheap."

Jake shook his head. "She's getting everything as free samples from her company."

"Now I'm doubly sorry for you, dude," Ben said. "Banging two women and getting free decorating."

"You know there's no such thing as a free lunch, right?" Jake added. "Anyway, I could use something to help me cope with all the craziness, like a pick-me-up, you know?"

Ben's eyes darted around the cafeteria before he leaned in and whispered, "Am I reading the tea leaves correctly here, bro? Because, aside from letting strangers grope your junk for a dollar, you're a fucking Eagle Scout."

"Do you have any of that stuff left?" Jake asked. "You know, the stuff you took from the truck?"

Ben glanced around the room and nodded. "I believe there might be a couple of snorts left."

"You took more than I thought," Jake observed. "Didn't you?"

An evil grin spread across Ben's face. "Perhaps."

Jake leaned back and said, "It's a wonder you and I aren't standing at the bottom of Lake Superior wearing our new cement Reeboks."

Ben leaned closer, his voice barely audible. "Shall we go back to my dorm and indulge?"

The idea tugged at Jake's vulnerable state of mind. "That might be exactly what I need right now. A little escape from reality."

"This will be another one of those wild, shared experiences we'll look back on fondly someday," Ben said with a wink.

After a heavy sigh, Jake said, "Okay, but just a small amount."

"Dude," Ben said, jumping up and hot to trot. "You talk like I don't know moderation."

37. Dumped

MUSIC pulsed through The Velvet Joystick, and the air was thick with tension as Brett Booth left the stage and made his way to the changing room. He steeled himself for a confrontation as Jake prepared for his next performance. "We need to talk," he demanded.

For days, Brett grappled with the painful loss of Sarah. The separation cut deep, and he couldn't bear the thought of her being with Jake Whitney, a guy he had considered a sorta-kinda friend until life took a cruel twist, turning an innocent bachelorette party into an occasion for betrayal. As Brett danced on the same stage as Jake each night, the cheers from the audience now felt hollow, and his heartache was his silent soundtrack.

Jake's eyes met Brett's, a mixture of surprise and apprehension in his gaze. "What's there to talk about?" he said, his voice tinged with defensiveness.

"I need to know why," Brett said.

Jake shrugged. "You'll have to ask Sarah."

"She meant everything to me," Brett confessed. "I need to know what you have that I don't."

Jake was about to say, "Tighter nuts," but he didn't want to add insult to the poor guy's injury. Instead, he said, "I didn't initiate it, Brett. I never intended to come between you two. She made the first move. My first concern was about you. No bullshit."

"Oh sure," Brett said. "Pull the other one, dude, it's got bells on it."

"Love is unpredictable," Jake said. "I'm sorry. I truly am."

"I've tried to talk to her, but she won't answer my calls or texts," Brett said through gritted teeth.

Jake's eyes narrowed. "Well, maybe that should tell you something."

Brett scoffed. "What's that supposed to mean?"

"It means that maybe she's moved on, and you should too."

Brett felt a surge of anger rise up in him. "Moved on? With you?"

Jake shrugged again. "She's a grown woman. She can make her own decisions."

"I need to see her," Brett said, his voice laced with desperation. "Please, Jake, will you just tell her that for me?"

Jake hesitated before finally speaking. "She's not going to want to talk to you, Brett."

Jake's words were like salt in his wounds. Brett clenched his teeth so hard they ached, and his fists tensed at his sides as he fought the urge to lunge at Jake. He knew he couldn't let his temper get the best of him. "I'd beat the shit out of you," he said, "but I'm a lover, not a fighter." He took a deep breath and leaned against the wall, trying to regain control of his temper.

"Glad to hear that," Jake said, "because you could definitely do me some serious damage. Look, I'm not proud of what happened. I had no intention of betraying our friendship or causing you pain. Sarah and I found ourselves in a situation, and things spiraled from there."

"A situation?" Brett rubbed a hand across his face, struggling to understand how things had come to this point. "I trusted you, Jake. I thought you were my friend. Friends don't seduce other friends' women."

Jake's face darkened with remorse. "I'm not making excuses, but sometimes, feelings and attraction are beyond our control. It's not as simple as 'resisting' or 'giving in.' I know that doesn't help."

"Doesn't help?" Brett let out a bitter laugh. "You've shattered my world, man." His emotions were a swirling vortex of confusion.

"I hope you can find it in your heart to forgive us both someday," Jake told him.

"Know what? It's actually all *my* fault, man," Brett said. "I had the brilliant idea to have the bachelorette bullshit here. I could fuckin' kick myself!"

The club continued to throb with music as Tony's heavy footsteps could be heard stomping down the hall. He was in a tirade, as usual, when he burst into the room.

"Hey, Jake! Where the fuck are you?" he screamed. "Why isn't your ass up on that stage?"

Jake rolled his eyes in frustration and did a last-minute check in the mirror. "Give me a minute, Tony."

Tony wagged a finger at Brett. "And your timin' was seriously off tonight, buddy," he snapped. "I could tell your head was a million miles away. The audience felt it, too. Or, more to the point, they *didn't* feel it."

As Jake headed for the stage, he extended his hand to Brett. "Again, I really am sorry," he said, but Brett turned away, ignoring him.

"You two can kiss and make up later," Tony bellowed. "Get out there, Jake."

Tony watched Jake jog toward the stage, then saw Brett gathering up his belongings and shoving them into a sports bag. "Where do you think you're goin'?"

"It's been nice, Tony," Brett said, continuing to pack.

"You have another set tonight," Tony barked.

"No, I don't." Brett conducted a final check of the area around him. "Studmuffins is hiring. And they have better benefits."

Tony looked like he was about to blow a gasket. "Studmuffins is a flea pit!"

Brett looked Tony straight in the eye. "Fire Jake, and I'll stay."

Tony looked at the floor and sighed. "No can do, kid," he said. "Jake's my main attraction, and you know that."

Brett gave Tony an affectionate tap on the shoulder. "Yeah, I know that," he mumbled, and walked toward the exit of The Velvet Joystick for the last time.

38. The Whole Nine Yards

"THE idiots who say money can't buy happiness must be shopping at the wrong stores," Veronica Marino remarked as she poured herself a bourbon. Her silk La Perla robe was unbelted and flapping open, revealing only skin underneath.

"Give me a sip of that," Jake said, reclining on the bed in a pair of red boxers, lost in thought.

She handed him the bottle. "I'm glad you finally decided to call me." Her tone was playful, but an underlying current of possessiveness was evident. "I figure you needed money, or you needed coke, or maybe you needed both?"

"I'm still figuring out what I need," he replied, sitting up and taking a swig. He could feel the familiar warmth of the alcohol easing the tension that had been building up inside him.

"What's bothering you tonight?" Veronica furrowed her brow and pursed her lips. "The past few times we've been together, you haven't been your perky self."

"There's never enough time, Ronnie," he sighed. "With work, and school, and, you know, the whole nine yards?"

She stirred her drink with her finger and then sucked it suggestively. "I never got that," she said. "The whole nine yards? What does it mean, anyway?"

"I think it means giving it your all," he explained. "You know, putting in the effort until you've gone *the whole nine yards*."

"Yeah, but the whole nine yards to, like, *where*? That's what I'm asking," she said. "Sorry, I didn't get a college diploma like you."

"I haven't earned it yet," he admitted, stifling a yawn. "And I won't if I don't straighten up."

"Who needs a college diploma when you've got other talents?" Veronica grabbed the bourbon bottle and poured another.

Jake's eyes roamed over her exposed body, feeling embarrassed by her casual abandon. "Close your robe," he said, averting his eyes and realizing she was his mother's age.

"You allergic to pussy all of a sudden?" she said. "Is being around all those naked men every night making you *gay,* little boy?"

Veronica leaned in and kissed him, her hands running through his hair. But then, as suddenly as it had started, she pulled away, a glint of something darker in her eyes.

"What's the matter?" he said.

"How about we ditch the Kool-Aid and get out the *adult* party favors?" she suggested.

He had made a vow with himself that same morning to make an effort to quit by taking one day at a time. "I think the bourbon is enough for now, thank you very much."

"Don't be a party pooper," Veronica said. "A snort will do us both a world of good."

Jake Whitney's life had taken an unexpected and dark turn. His involvement with Veronica, which had begun as a glamorous escape, had spiraled into a nightmare. The extravagant lifestyle she had introduced him to had included the excesses of food, drink, and drugs, with one vice in particular that would lead him down a treacherous path. After his bad-boy dorm room experiment with Ben Mendelsen, it wasn't long before the bony claw of cocaine had Jake by the throat and would not let go. He couldn't remember the last time he had slept or even eaten. All he could think about was the next hit, the next thrill, the next moment of ecstasy.

Veronica handed Jake a mirror holding a line of powder. He leaned over and snorted the line, feeling the rush of euphoria and energy that started in his toes and shot up to his brain. He pictured that carnival game where you swing a mallet and it rings a bell.

She grinned at him, her eyes dark with desire. "That's it, baby," she murmured, her hand tracing down his smooth chest. "Let's forget about everything else and just live in the moment."

The sensation of the drug was too tempting, and the allure of Veronica's world had become increasingly difficult to resist. Cocaine offered a temporary escape from the mounting stress and anxiety of trying to balance college, work, and the demands of both Sarah and his secret relationship with Veronica. Occasional indulgences had a way of quickly escalating into increasingly dangerous habits, and coke had become his crutch, with Veronica his enabler. The drug was free, free, *free*, but it had him dancing to her tune and he was forced to service her royally at the snap of her expensively manicured fingers.

Jake flopped backward on the bed and waited for the full effect to take hold. It also loosened his tongue. "By the way, Ronnie, I think we need to cool things."

"Cool things?" she asked. "What are you talking about?"

"I don't know if I can do this anymore," he confessed. "It's not healthy for either of us."

"How is it not healthy?" She scraped together another line with a credit card and snorted it.

"I keep looking over my shoulder," he said, "scared shitless I'll end up like Marco at the end of Pier 27."

"I make those decisions, sweet cheeks, not you." Veronica's voice rose in anger. "You know I'm never gonna let you just up and leave me, so forget it!"

She pulled him closer, her breath hot against his ear. He trailed his fingertips down the curve of her neck, sending shivers down her spine. Their lips met in a fevered kiss and their tongues danced a tango of desire.

Veronica let the robe fall. "Take me, Jake," she whispered, her voice hoarse.

He staggered to his feet and pulled off his boxers, his erection standing straight up and flat against his belly. Coke had that effect on him, for a while, anyway. He had to strike while the iron was *hard*, and he pulled her close, his hands running over her body.

"I want to feel every inch of it," she gasped, a hand gripping each of his butt cheeks to pull him closer.

Jake took a deep breath to steady himself, and then pushed forward full of purpose. He had allowed himself to fall deeper into Veronica's world, a world that was dangerous and destructive but also utterly thrilling. He knew deep down that he should walk away, that he was risking everything he cared about, but he couldn't bring himself to do it. The drugs, the booze, the sex, were all so dirty and seductive, not the squeaky clean life he had with a nice girl like Sarah Miller.

"You're gonna kill me, Ronnie." He grunted like an animal with every thrust. "I swear you're going to fucking kill me."

"I'm not going all Marco Santangelo on you quite yet, sweet cheeks," she purred. "After all, you're the life support system for that gorgeous cock of yours. Now give it to me deep, baby. I want the whole nine yards."

He was so caught up in the moment, it wasn't until the following day that he recalled her muttering something cryptic about Marco Santangelo.

164

39. Interior Motives

WHILE Jake remained occupied with his job, schoolwork, and the undisclosed extracurricular activities he wisely kept to himself, Sarah devoted her time to a demanding career at the design firm, Interior Motives. Lately, the ticking of the clock on her desk appeared to have grown louder, a constant reminder of the minutes slipping through her fingers. Sarah's long hours at the office were not only a reflection of her commitment to her job but also a desperate attempt to drown out the noise of her inner turmoil. She eagerly anticipated those rare moments when she could focus on her own pleasures, like searching for furniture and other decorating freebies to spruce up their studio apartment.

One sunny Friday afternoon, Sarah lunched with her colleague Melissa at a cozy cafe near her workplace, and Melissa sensed something had changed in Sarah's life.

"I just want to make a name for myself, you know?" Sarah said while poking at her salad. "I want to live up to the potential my professors saw in me. I was a star pupil, a straight-A student, and I earned a scholarship to one of the top design schools in the country. My professors praised my innate talent and predicted a bright future for me in the world of interior design. And here I am, drowning in a sea of stress and self-doubt. It's a far cry from the grandeur I had envisioned, I'll tell you that."

"You've achieved so much already," reassured Melissa, a talented designer herself. "You're being especially hard on yourself."

"The clock is ticking, Melissa." Sarah leaned back and chewed her food, deep in thought. It was evident something was bothering her. "It's time to balance the demands of my career with the dreams that are still alive inside me."

Melissa raised her latte and exclaimed, "Amen to that. If only it were easier."

Sarah's professional life had turned into a whirlwind of deadlines, client meetings, and endless revisions. Juggling high-profile projects while ensuring Interior Motives' success had begun to take its toll. Sarah was a perfectionist; every detail of every project had to be flawless. This was both a strength and a curse, as she pushed herself to her limits, often losing sleep and missing out on important moments with Jake.

"I thought I'd be working on grand projects, living in opulence, and maybe even having my own design studio by now, transforming lavish penthouses and luxury hotels into works of art," Sarah said. "And here I am redecorating a seven-hundred square foot studio apartment for free, hunting for bargains, and squeezing the last drop out of every dime to make a cramped space feel like a home."

"Maybe you need to reevaluate your priorities," Melissa suggested. "Part of your problem is that you're a control freak. Start delegating tasks to your team and be more of a mentor to your junior designers, empowering them to excel."

"Here's to all those corporate buzzwords," Sarah toasted.

Melissa shrugged. "Well, those corporate buzzwords are the world we live in, and they aren't going away."

"I mean, will I achieve recognition by nurturing the talents of those around me?" Sarah pondered. "Maybe with Jake's support and a fresh outlook, right?"

"Suit yourself, Sarah," Melissa sighed, taking a sip of her latte. "Maybe I should keep my big mouth shut, but your attitude has changed since..." She hesitated and looked away.

"Since what?" Sarah knew what Melissa was about to say.

Melissa turned back and looked at Sarah with a soulful expression. "Since...Since *Jake*."

"I figured as much," Sarah said with a heavy sigh. "I knew you didn't like him, and you think I made a terrible mistake."

"You two just seem so different, with different goals," Melissa said. "He doesn't even have a degree yet."

Sarah rolled her eyes. "I know, I know. He's not exactly the corporate type. But he makes me happy, and that's all that matters."

"Is that true?" Melissa raised her eyebrows. "Is it really all that matters?"

Sarah frowned. "What do you mean?"

"Are you truly happy with where you are in life? Are you happy with Jake?" Melissa asked.

"I can't lie." Sarah hesitated, feeling a sudden lump in her throat. "I've been thinking about that a lot lately."

Melissa took a bite of her burger. "I knew there was something on your mind."

There was a long moment of silence between the two women as they focused on lunch. Sarah knew Melissa was only looking out for her, but her sudden questioning of Sarah's relationship with Jake had taken her off guard. She knew Jake was not the typical guy her colleagues would approve of, but Sarah had always been one to go against the grain.

"Look, I love Jake," Sarah said, her voice gentle. "He's not perfect, but neither am I. But he supports me and my dreams, and that's all that matters."

Melissa nodded, seeming to accept Sarah's response. "Just remember, Sarah, you deserve the world. Don't settle for anything less."

Those words lingered in Sarah's mind as she returned to her office. Lately, something had shifted, something she couldn't quite put her finger on. Was it because they were both so busy with their own separate lives they hardly had time for each other? Or was it something deeper, something she had been ignoring for far too long?

Sarah took a deep breath and turned her attention back to her work. She had a project deadline looming, and she couldn't afford to let her personal life distract her. But even as she immersed herself in her work, it was impossible to shake the feeling something was amiss with Jake Whitney.

40. Not So Very Funny

AS LEO Shaw walked up to the stage, his heart clicked a mile a second. The bright spotlight made it hard to see the audience, but he could feel their expectant eyes on him. He clutched the microphone like a lifeline, taking a deep breath before launching into his set.

"Good evening, ladies and gentlemen, and thank you for coming out tonight. Full disclosure, I am not a full-time comedian. That might come as a surprise, I know, but actually, most nights I am an exotic dancer. That's a polite word for a stripper. Yes, ladies and gentlemen, if you'd like to see what's underneath these pants, just hop on over to The Velvet Joystick, and you will find out. But bring plenty of dollar bills."

Leo's face reddened, and he stuttered, feeling like he was suffocating.

"I've been dancing for years, and let me tell you, it's a lot like dating. You start with some fancy moves, and if you're lucky, you end with a standing ovation in your pants. When you're a dancer, people expect you to be light on your feet. I tell them, 'I'm practically weightless when I'm dancing, but ask me to carry groceries, and I'll need a forklift!' But I'm always ready to bust a move, you know? Even in a grocery store, you might find me in the cereal aisle, hoping some old lady will stuff a dollar bill in my Cheerios!"

Leo felt defeated, humiliated, and overwhelmed by self-doubt.

"Just to keep life interesting, as well as buy food, I work at a dollar store during the day, which is like being in a never-ending episode of *The Price Is Right*. 'Come on down!' And the price is always one dollar! A customer once asked me if we had a loyalty program at the dollar store. I said, 'Absolutely! Spend a buck and you get a dollar's worth of loyalty!' I learned that anything can be an impulse purchase. I went in for a candy bar and came out with a bag full of glow-in-the-dark shoelaces, half a dozen rubber ducks, and a carton of plastic forks."

Leo tried to switch gears and share personal anecdotes, hoping to connect with the audience on a more heartfelt level.

"And being single, well, I know a lot about plastic forks. What can I say? That's my good silverware. Ah, yes, I uttered the curs-*ed* word: *single*. Being single is like being the last slice of pizza at a party. Everyone wants it, but no one is ready to take a chance and commit. That's why I thought stripping would help my love life. You can see the goods before you purchase them. You can even squeeze the fruit if you like, no problem. It'll cost you a dollar, but it's a better value than what you get for a buck at the dollar sore, believe me."

He lowered the microphone, his shoulders slumping in defeat. At least he gets hoots, hollers, and applause at The Velvet Joystick.

"Thank you," he said quietly. "You've been a great audience."

The disdain from the thin crowd hung in the air like a thick fog, and Leo made a fast retreat from the stage, his head hanging low. The dream of being a stand-up comedian had crumbled before his eyes.

As he headed for the dressing room, a familiar figure standing in the back caught his eye. "Jake? Is that you?"

Jake stepped out of the shadows. "Hey, man," he said. "Nice job."

"I should have taken my clothes off," Leo said.

"You were fine," Jake said. "The audience was lousy."

"I appreciate the kindness," Leo said, "but I know how bad I was. It's amazing how your perspective changes when you stand in front of a bunch of strangers."

"You're just finding that out?" Jake said.

Leo chuckled. "I guess I am. I thought I could handle it, but it's tougher than I imagined."

Jake patted Leo's back. "Listen, man. You've got talent. You just need to find better material."

"I saw the day approaching when I couldn't dance anymore," Leo sighed. "I have nothing to fall back on, Jake. I'm older than you. The years are zooming by."

Jake nodded. "I know, Leo. But you're not alone. We all have moments of doubt and fear. But you're a survivor, man. Don't give up on your dream."

Leo looked at Jake, his eyes shining with gratitude. "Thanks, that means a lot."

"Let's grab a drink," Jake said. "And not at The Velvet Joystick, either."

"Deal," Leo said, "but I'm buying."

Jake gave him a hug. "We can talk about your next set."

"There won't be a next set," Leo said, shaking his head. "I am done, done, *done* with standup." He made a fist, then splayed his fingers open. "*Poof*!"

"Have you ever considered writing?" Jake asked.

Leo snorted. "Writing? What would I write about?"

"How about your experiences as a dancer, a stripper?" Jake suggested. "Life at The Velvet Joystick is a situation comedy gold mine."

Leo smiled and nodded. "That's a fact."

"Start by making some notes," Jake explained. "Then create an outline. Let it simmer in your mind for a while, then roll up your sleeves and have at it."

"A comic novel," Leo said. "Heck, yeah."

"There ya go!"

"I think I might give it a whirl."

"And I have a title for it," Jake said.

"What?"

"*Show It To Me.*"

"I fucking *love* that!" Leo said.

41. Confrontation

SARAH'S day began like any other. After Jake had left for an early class, she savored her morning coffee in the peaceful quiet. She loved Jake, but she also took pleasure in those moments where she could gather her thoughts and prepare to face the non-stop chaos that greeted her when she stepped into the offices of Interior Motives. As the sun streamed through the window, casting a warm glow throughout the small apartment, Sarah stretched and gave herself kudos for the happy changes she had made in the decor of their apartment. So far, it was coming together nicely.

The sudden, unexpected knock on the door made her jump. Such sounds were rare in the quiet, secluded building, and she had already delivered the rent check in person. Setting her coffee down, she peered through the peephole and saw a woman with an air of authority, dressed in a tailored suit that was somewhat out of place in the working-class setting. The woman's stern expression sent shivers down Sarah's spine, and she hesitated before cautiously unlocking the door. Surely, a salesperson would reflect a cheerier disposition than this.

As soon as the door was slightly open, the woman stormed in, her stiletto heels echoing on the bare floor. "You must be Sarah," she declared, her eyes locking onto Sarah's with an unsettling intensity. "I'm Veronica. Veronica *Marino*."

Sarah's heart raced as she nodded, her voice trembling. "What do you want?"

"I don't expect he's told you about me." Veronica's gaze softened a bit as she replied, "I want you to know the truth about Jake Whitney. The complete *unvarnished* truth."

Sarah's mind swirled as she tried to comprehend what was happening. "What truth are you talking about?"

With a cold, calculating smile, Veronica continued, "Jake and I have been, to put it delicately, well, we've been *intimate* for quite some time, which is putting it mildly."

Sarah's world crumbled around her. "Who are you again?"

"I told you who I was, honey," Veronica snapped. "Your boy has been leading a double life."

"No," Sarah gasped. "That can't be true."

"It always amazes me how ignorant some women are, or pretend to be." Veronica cast a disparaging look around the room.

Sarah took a deep breath. "Please leave."

"You're the one who'll be leaving," Veronica hissed. "Would you like me to describe his body to you in detail? Maybe that will convince you. Let's see, where should I start? Okay, there's that tiny little birthmark right under his..."

"Shut up!" Sarah struggled to breathe. "Get out of my house!"

"You call this a house? Supposedly, you're a decorator, right?" Veronica sneered as she sized up the apartment. "Seriously? He leaves my elegant bed and comes home to *this*? How depressing."

Tears welled up in Sarah's eyes. "Jake loves me."

Veronica's tone turned menacing as she leaned in closer. "Oh, sweetheart, he might *say* he loves you, but he's been playing you all along. And you don't want to know what will happen if you cross me."

"I told you to leave." Fear coursed through Sarah's veins as she stammered. "Do you...want me...to call the police?"

"Go for it, sweetie! My husband *owns* the cops!" Veronica leaned back, her face a mask of cold determination. "Let's just say the Marinos are not the kind of folks you want to mess with. We have connections, and neither one of us will hesitate to make both of your lives very uncomfortable if you don't comply."

Sarah's heart sank as she contemplated the implications of what Veronica was saying. She had no doubt these were not empty threats. "Comply with what exactly?"

"Pack up your things, honey, and get your homogenized little ass out of Jake's life," Veronica said, maintaining her cold, hard stare.

"What does your husband have to say about all this?" Sarah stood tall and stared right back. "Does he approve of your extracurricular activities?"

Veronica responded with a mix of desperation and defiance. "That is none of your goddamn business. Jake has become part of a dangerous world, and if he decides to leave, well, I won't just let him go."

"I won't let him go either," Sarah said.

"I suggest you tell Jake about my little visit and see what he says." Veronica's smirk reminded Sarah of the face of the Devil. "Trust me, he's in way over his head."

Sarah remained resolute. "Jake is strong, and your threats won't keep him tied to that destructive life."

"Sorry to be the bearer of bad news," Veronica said, as she turned toward the door and put her hand on the knob. "He's a weak, scared little boy, but I have to admit, he does *fuck* me beautifully!"

• • • •

42. Biggest Loser

"I WISH you could call my dad for me," Ben said, his voice quivering with emotion. He was sitting next to Jake on his unmade dorm room bed, ankle-deep in a sea of trash, dirty laundry, and despair.

"You're going to have to face him sometime," Jake replied, a note of concern in his voice. "Talking to him on the phone is the least of your worries now."

Ben's eyes filled with tears as he contemplated the mess he had made of his life. "How did I let this monkey on my back consume me?" He fell backward on the bed, as if the weight of his addiction was pressing him into the mattress.

Jake had his own demons to wrestle with, and he empathized with Ben's pain. "I'm no one to preach," he admitted. "I'm pretty deep in trouble myself."

Ben managed a weak smile, despite his dire circumstances. "You may be balls deep in Veronica Marino," he said with a touch of bitterness, "but you're still in school. There's hope for you."

Jake pondered for a moment before making a suggestion. "Have you considered going to the dean and begging and pleading for a second chance?"

Ben sat up, his face reddening with shame and anger. "Dude, I'd get down on my knees and suck him dry if I knew it might get him to reconsider."

Jake winced at Ben's choice of words, but he understood the depths of Ben's desperation. "Alright, let's not get carried away," Jake said. "But we won't rule out that option quite yet."

Ben wiped away a tear. "I had twenty thousand bucks in my hands, and I let it go. Half that money was rightfully yours, too, and you gave it to me. There's no hope for me, bro. That's all there is to it. No hope at all."

Jake leaned in, his voice filled with determination. "First, we need to get you into rehab. It's the first step to conquering your addiction. And as for school, maybe we can talk to some of your professors, explain your situation, and see if there's any way they can help you catch up, maybe put in a good word."

Ben felt a glimmer of hope amidst the darkness that had consumed him. "Rehab sounds scary. I don't know if I can do it."

Jake patted his friend on the back. "We'll support each other through this. And as for your dad, I'll help you make that call so you won't have to face it alone."

"I don't know why you have anything to do with me." Ben looked at Jake with guilt in his eyes. "I've been such a lousy friend, Jake, a real lousy friend."

"Why do you say that?" Jake asked, even though he sort of agreed. "Because you blew the money, you mean?"

"I've been a burden to you, man. Dragging you down with me. I don't know how to repay you."

Jake put his hand on Ben's shoulder. "You don't have to repay me. That's what friends are for."

Ben wiped his nose on his sleeve. "I don't deserve a friend like you, Jake."

Jake shook his head. "Don't be ridiculous. We all make mistakes. The important thing is to learn from them and move forward."

Ben sighed. "If only it were that easy."

"Oh, it's not going to be easy," Jake warned him.

"I've been a lousy friend even before that. I never really listened to your problems or cared about your feelings. I was so self-absorbed in my own issues that I didn't see how much you were struggling, too."

Jake shook his head. "We were both going through our own stuff, man. It's not your fault."

"But I should have been there for you," Ben said, his voice cracking with emotion. "Like you're here for me now."

"You are here for me, too," Jake said. "Just by talking to me, sharing your struggles, and letting me help you."

Ben felt a small glimmer of hope. "Okay, let's do this. Rehab first, then school."

Jake gave him a determined nod. "That's the plan, man."

Ben let out a big sigh and sniffed. "Tell you what, bro. To pay you back, I'll go stick it in Veronica Marino just to give you a break."

Jake said, "Well, be my guest and have at it, bro!" as they both dissolved in laughter.

43. Painful Choice

WE. NEED. TO. TALK.

The four most ominous words in any relationship never bode well, and when Jake heard Sarah utter them, he knew.

He. Just. Knew.

Sarah sat on the couch with a tense expression on her face. The TV was on, but she had no idea what was playing, nor did she care. The background murmurs of indistinguishable voices were preferable to the soft hum of city traffic outside. She had been anxiously waiting all night for Jake's return from The Velvet Joystick, the weight of Veronica Marino's visit still heavy on her mind. She had picked up her phone at least a dozen times during the day to call or text him, knowing the only right way to confront him with the earth-shaking revelation was to do it face-to-face.

Finally, Jake entered with a smile on his face, but the dour mood in the apartment was thick with trepidation. He didn't receive the usual greeting from Sarah followed by a routine hug and kiss, and his concerned "Hey, what's going on? Is everything okay?" was met with ominous silence. A verbal answer to his question was no longer necessary when he walked over and was struck by the seriousness evident in her eyes.

Sarah took a deep breath, turned off the TV, and tried to steady her nerves. "Jake," she said, her voice tinged with a mix of frustration and disappointment, then uttering those painful four words.

Jake's brow furrowed, and he took a seat across from her, curiosity piqued. "Of course, what's on your mind?"

Sarah's eyes bore into his as she spoke. "Veronica Marino came to visit me today," she said, her tone heavy with accusation. "She told me everything, Jake."

Jake's face paled as the weight of her words sank in. Even though he had been dreading this moment, it still came as a shock. "Sarah, I can explain. Please..."

Sarah cut him off, her voice trembling with anger. "Explain what, Jake? Explain how you've been lying to me all this time? How you made me believe you were faithful while secretly having an affair with another woman behind my back? And what a woman! A gangster's wife! Am I in a *movie* or what? I'm shattered, Jake! Shattered!"

Jake hung his head, unable to meet Sarah's gaze. "I never meant for things to get so complicated. I was afraid of losing you, and I thought I could handle both relationships. But I was wrong, and I'm so sorry for hurting you."

Tears welled up in Sarah's eyes, but she refused to let them fall. "Sorry isn't enough, Jake. I deserve honesty and respect in a relationship, and you've shown me neither. I can't continue to live like this."

Jake reached out, his hand hovering as if to comfort her. But she pulled away, her resolve firm. "I'm moving out. I can't stay here knowing the truth. I need to heal and rebuild my trust with someone who truly deserves it."

Silence hung in the air, heavy and suffocating. Sarah's decision had been made, and the consequences of his actions were sinking in for Jake. He watched as she stood up and headed toward their bedroom to pack. Dishonesty had come at a steep price.

"I love you, Sarah," he replied, his voice cracking with emotion, "and it tears me apart to see how I've put you in this position."

Sarah turned toward him, her voice cracking. "You *love* me? Seriously? I'm supposed to believe that?"

"This all started before I met you and it had strings attached that I couldn't sever," he said. "Threats were made. Very serious threats."

Sarah's eyes were cold. "Threats were made today, too."

"I can't imagine my life without you," he said.

Sarah shook her head. "Were you thinking that when you climbed into bed with her? I have my own safety and well-being to consider," she said. "I need to leave this ugly ...*thing*... behind me."

Jake sighed and ran a hand through his hair. "I promise you, Sarah," he said, his voice filled with remorse, "I'll do whatever it takes to make things right. I'll cut ties with Veronica, and I'll make sure you stay safe."

"It's not just about Veronica," Sarah said, her voice softer now. "What else have you kept from me? It's about the breach of trust, the secrecy, and the lies. I don't think we can ever rebuild an honest relationship on top of that."

Jake nodded, understanding the gravity of the situation. "I can't erase what I've done, but I'll do whatever it takes to earn back your trust."

"I need time and space," she said. "I need to get away from you."

The words stung, and Jake winced. "Even if it takes a lifetime," he said, knowing at that moment there was nothing more he could say or do to change Sarah's mind.

Sarah came out of the bedroom with a small suitcase. "I'll come back and get the rest of my things when you're not here," she said. "I'll leave the key on the table." She left the apartment, her suitcase light, her heart heavy with the burden of a broken relationship.

The lonesome hum of city traffic floating through the open window was all Jake could hear, so he turned on the TV, hoping it would drown out the deafening quiet.

44. One is a Lonely Number

THE relentless sound of icy rain pelting the apartment windows only deepened Jake's already sullen mood. In the days following Sarah's departure, he found himself sinking further into a pit of loneliness and despair. With each passing hour, the weight of his actions bore down on him, and he yearned for the comforting presence of Sarah. But it was the cold, empty bed at night that tormented him the most, where he lay staring at the ceiling, yearning for the chance to rewind his life and undo the mistakes that had driven her away.

Jake had called off work and missed classes for two consecutive days. It was high time he roused himself from his depression. "Damn," he muttered while stretching and yawning, realizing it was already Friday.

His shift at the bar loomed, and it promised to be particularly demanding. Tony was struggling to recruit new dancers due to fierce competition from Studmuffins, and the bar's dance team had dwindled down to Ethan, Leo, and himself, and Jake had a strong hunch that Leo was on the verge of leaving as well. To add to the pressure, he had a major psychology exam the next morning, and the weight of the material burdened him.

In desperate need of a pick-me-up to get him through the torturous days, Jake had been taking the occasional snort of cocaine to maintain his energy. When Ben agreed to get clean, he had entrusted Jake to dispose of what remained of his stash, but Jake had kept it for his own use, using it sparingly to avoid having to ask Veronica for more.

As the first hit of cocaine surged through his veins, a momentary euphoria overtook the despair that had been his constant companion. It felt so good he indulged in another hit. And another. Okay, maybe just one more.

Soon, Jake couldn't feel his own feet. How would he manage to get to the bar in this state? He needed the money from tonight's shift to make rent, and he couldn't afford to lose his job. Jake stumbled through his apartment, knocking over one of Sarah's artsy-fartsy new lamps. "Good riddance," he mumbled, taking a deep breath to steady himself. His heart was racing and he was sweating profusely.

With one hand on the wall to balance, Jake managed to make it into the shower, letting the water pound on his head, but he still felt as if he were soaring to the peak of Mount Everest, and climbing ever higher.

Struggling to focus, he squinted at his phone screen, desperately trying to locate the Uber app. After a few minutes of fumbling, he finally found the app and ordered a ride to the bar.

The ride had been a blur, with Jake barely registering the outside world. As he stumbled out of the Uber and through the front door of The Velvet Joystick, the barrage of flashing lights and thumping music caused him to panic. The bar was already packed with a lively crowd, and Jake took a moment to compose himself before making his way to the back room to change.

Ethan was already there to witness Jake's disheveled state, and rushed to help him settle on a bench. "What happened, buddy?" he inquired, concern lacing his voice.

Ethan's voice sounded to Jake like it was coming from the bottom of a metal trash can. Jake struggled to focus, the effects of the drugs muddling his senses. The distant thump of music and the crowd's roar sounded worlds away. He took a few deep breaths, trying to push away the haze that clouded his mind.

Tony, in his usual frenzied state, appeared abruptly. "Leo called off, the bastard! So it's all you guys tonight," he growled. "Again! Are youse two gonna be able to handle this here crowd?"

"We'll be fine, Tony," Ethan assured him, attempting to conceal Jake's condition.

Tony glanced at Jake sitting slouched with closed eyes, and wasn't fooled. "What's up with him?"

"Rough day at, uh, school, not much sleep," Ethan haltingly explained.

"Well, give him a hand getting undressed," Tony told him. "I'm countin' on youse two!" With a grumble and a glance at his watch, Tony vanished as swiftly as he arrived.

Ethan attempted to rouse Jake. "Hey, Jake? Hey, buddy?"

Jake's eyes flickered open. "Where the fuck am I?" he moaned.

"You're at the club," Ethan said. "I don't know how on God's green earth you got yourself here, but you're here."

"What...club?" Jake's head thumped against the wall.

"The Velvet Joystick," Ethan told him.

"Oh, shit," Jake said in a moment of clarity. "Gimme a hand, will ya?"

"Are you going to be able to dance?"

"Sure, sure," he said, but his eyes were still closed. "I'll be fine in a minute. Or three."

Ethan helped Jake out of his jacket and then pulled his t-shirt over his head. "Scooch your butt up so I can take off your pants."

Jake rose off the bench about an inch, enough for Ethan to pull off his sweatpants. "I owe you one, bud," he said, before flopping back down on the bench.

"You're gonna have to do that again for me to get your underwear off," Ethan said, but he put that task off until he had Jake's sneakers and socks off first.

"My tongue feels like the Sahara desert, man," Jake said. "Can you get me a drink of water?"

"Coming right up." Ethan filled a plastic cup with water from the cooler, and by the time he returned, Jake was on his feet.

Jake downed the water, feeling the cold liquid soothe his burning throat. The effects of the cocaine were still coursing through his veins, but he could feel himself gradually coming back to reality. He leaned against the wall, taking deep breaths, and tried to steady himself.

"Where's wasisname Leo?" Jake asked, his voice rough.

"He called in sick," Ethan replied. "He's been talking about quitting for a while now. I think he's just about had it with this place."

"Can't blame him," Jake muttered, trying his best to push away the feeling of overwhelming exhaustion.

"You still need a hand getting ready?"

Jake nodded. "If...you don't...mind."

They say everything comes to those who will but wait. Ethan found himself in a situation he had fantasized about, dreamed about, and stayed awake nights wondering how he might make it happen, and here it was handed to him on a silver g-string, with Jake granting permission no less.

"Hot damn!" Ethan muttered to himself as he slid Jake Whitney's undershorts down to his ankles. The sight of Jake's naked body sent Ethan's pulse racing. He'd seen it many times before, of course, but this view was *oh so very up close and personal.* Ethan wondered if Jake would be too out of it to remember any of it.

Jake moaned, "Where's my wadchamacallit thong thingee?"

"I'll put it on you in a second," Ethan said. "You okay, buddy?"

"Yeah, yeah," Jake responded with a gentle snore. "I just need...a little...ya know...whatever."

Ethan only needed a little, ya know, whatever, too, and he couldn't resist the temptation to run his hands over Jake's smooth body, feeling his muscles tense under his touch. Although Jake's penis was soft, it was still Jake Whitney's one and only impressive penis, and Ethan knew this was a once in a lifetime opportunity he would regret letting slip away.

With the world frozen in an extraordinary moment, Ethan chose to preserve it for the future. After all, he required more than a mere memory of the occasion to satisfy his lonely nights, so he reached into the pocket of his pants hanging on the hook above and pulled out his phone.

"Hey! What was that *flash*?" Jake asked, stretching and flexing and almost ready to rejoin the living.

"Come on boys! Let's move it!" Tony shouted from the bar, sparing Ethan an explanation.

With his thong securely in place, Jake stumbled out of the back room and onto the stage. The bright lights blinded him for a few moments, but he quickly adjusted. The music was loud and the crowd was rowdy, waving their money in the air and shouting for Jake to come closer, closer, *closer,* but not nearly as close as Ethan had been.

• • • •

45. There's No Place Like Home

TONY Gaudio made the decision to shut down The Velvet Joystick during the week between Christmas and New Year's to give the place a refresh in a halfhearted attempt to bring the bar up to speed with Studmuffins, which, business-wise, had been eating his lunch. The rival club was banging the drum for a pull-out-the-stop New Year's Eve bash for which Tony had neither the budget nor the staff to compete with.

The hiatus gave Jake the perfect excuse to get outta Dodge and spend the Christmas holidays with his parents. He hadn't been back home since school started in September.

The only wrinkle in his plan was his parents' excitement about the prospect of meeting Sarah, who was originally supposed to join Jake for the holiday. He hadn't told them yet about the change of plan, and he wrestled with telling them the truth and throwing a damper over the holiday festivities. He chose to tell them that Sarah had an unexpected family emergency that forced her to cancel, which would delay having to explain to his parents why she left him. Yes, their only child was getting naked in public for money, sleeping with a gangster's wife, consuming rivers of alcohol, ingesting enormous quantities of drugs, and, in his spare time, running illegal deliveries for the mob. Mom and Dad would be so proud of their little boy they would most likely need hospitalization and years of therapy to recover.

"We can't wait to meet her," Jakes's mother said, "but there's always next time."

Jake's parents sat across from him in the cozy living room, the aroma of freshly baked apple pie filling the air.

"Yeah, it's a real bummer," Jake said, twirling his fork in his pie. "But at least I get to spend some quality time with you guys."

He hadn't missed the way his mother's eyes bored into him, as if she was searching for something beneath the surface. He hoped she wouldn't press the matter further because he wasn't in the habit of lying to his parents, which wasn't the same thing as not telling them something that might upset them.

His father, oblivious to the tension in the room, asked, "So, how's work going, son? It's only part time, right, so's not to add stress on your studies?"

"Yeah, it's going well," Jake said, forcing a smile and nodding. "I make overpriced fancy coffees for people, so what's to stress about?" He shifted in his seat, trying to ease the tightness in his chest. The weight of his lies was suffocating him, and he couldn't wait to get out of there.

His father cleared his throat and leaned forward. "Everything okay, son? You seem a bit, well, distracted."

Jake gulped, his nerves jangling like a live wire. He fidgeted with his fork and couldn't bear to look his father in the eye. "I'm just tired, Dad," he said, his voice barely above a whisper. "It's been a long semester, and work has been busy."

His father nodded slowly, not quite convinced. "Well, you know you can always talk to us. We're here for you, no matter what."

His father's words made Jake feel worse, and his stomach churned with guilt, knowing he would never be able to tell them the truth. He couldn't wait to leave and get back to his life in the city, because no matter how long he had managed on his own as a functioning adult, the moment he stepped back into his parents' home he became a helpless, mewling, puking infant once again.

That evening, after trimming the tree with his mother as his father snoozed away in his recliner just as he did when Jake was small, Jake returned to his old room furnished with the same IKEA knock-it-together-yourself stuff from his teen years, The Clash posters still taped on the wall.

He flopped onto the twin-sized bed, the springs creaking under his weight. His mind raced with thoughts of Sarah, the Velvet Joystick, and the dangerous situations he found himself in on a regular basis. He couldn't keep this up forever, he knew that, but the thrill of it all kept him coming back for more. The highs of performing on stage, the lure of the seedy underbelly of the city, it was all too seductive to resist. But he couldn't keep lying to his parents, pretending to be someone he wasn't. It was exhausting, and he knew it was only a matter of time before the truth came out.

As he settled into the twin bed, the memories of his past came flooding back, and he couldn't help but feel a pang of nostalgia for the way his life used to be. He closed his eyes and let out a heavy sigh, feeling the weight of his secrets pressing down on him once again. He wondered if his parents would still love him if they knew about his life of addiction, sex, and danger.

As he lay there, staring up at the ceiling, he heard a knock at the door.

"Jake? Can I come in?"

It was his mother's voice, and she sounded troubled. He quickly sat up, wiping the tears from his eyes. "Yeah, Mom, come on in," he said, trying to sound casual.

His mother entered looking pale as a ghost. Her trembling hand clutched her cell phone. "Jake?" she said in a hoarse whisper.

"What is it, Mom?" Apparently someone close had died, he was certain of it. Don't those tragedies always seem to happen around the holidays? He braced himself for bad news.

His mother turned the screen of the phone toward him. "Can you explain this to me, son?"

His heart dropped and a cold, clammy sweat broke out all over his body. There on his mother's phone glowed a crystal clear image showing him stark naked and leaning against the wall in the dressing room at The Velvet Joystick while Ethan Lopez swirled his tongue hungrily around Jake's flaccid, but still impressive, penis.

"LOOK on the bright side," Tony said, holding the phone close to his face to examine the video. "At least you ain't *hard*."

"Gee, thanks for putting it into perspective, Tony," Jake said. "That makes me feel *sooo* much better."

"What's this thing here?" Tony asked, pointing to a caption underneath the video: #CaughtOffGuard.

"That's called a hashtag," Jake explained. "Sorta like, 'Come check out this dude in his natural state'. Nice, huh?"

"So there's more?" Tony asked. "Pictures, I mean?"

"Hell, yes, there are more pictures!" Jake said. "There's a dozen lovely glamour poses from my toes to my nose."

Tony handed the phone back to Jake. "You could always say you wasn't enjoyin' it." He shrugged. "That's all I'm sayin'"

"I *wasn't* enjoying it!" Jake exclaimed. "I didn't even know it was *happening*!"

"So say it's not you," Tony suggested. "There's an age-old defense system called deny, deny, *deny*."

Jake shook his head. "It's too late for that."

"It's never too late for *nothin'*, and don't let it bother you, kid," Tony said. "I've walked in on a whole lot worse over the years, believe you me." He had a cloth in each hand as he wiped down the bar, reminding Jake of Mr. Miyagi in *The Karate Kid*, because in his own peculiar way, Tony was Jake's Mr. Miyagi.

"Don't let it bother me?" Jake chuckled. "My parents think I'm *gay* now, and they are certain I made up a fake girlfriend."

"Hey, you're a young, good lookin' guy," Tony said, dusting a few bottles. "What do they expect? That maybe you're a monk?"

"You should have heard them." Jake rolled his eyes and sighed. "They can't believe they raised a son who would do something like that

that! How could I treat them this way? Their hearts are broken! Well, maybe my mother's heart is broken. My father doesn't have a heart."

"A little bit of an overreaction," Tony said. "Dontcha think?"

Jake cradled his face in his hands. "Imagine if they knew the *whole* story?"

"Can you sue over somethin' like this?" Tony asked. "You know, postin' nudies of somebody's person without their permission?"

"You talkin', like, revenge porn?"

"Is that what they're callin' it these days?" Tony shrugged. "I remember snappin' Polaroids of Mary Lou Artelli polishin' Jimmy Nolan's knob."

Jake nodded. "Welcome to the world of ones and zeroes."

Tony looked puzzled. "What'd you ever do to Ethan he should take revenge on you like this?"

"As much as I'd like to choke him for doing it," Jake said. "I think it was an accident."

"An accident?" Tony asked. "Like how an accident?"

"I think he probably meant to send it to just one person," Jake conjectured.

"That's bad enough!" Tony said.

"I know, whatever." Jake shrugged. "Bragging rights, I suppose. He probably clicked 'reply all' or some other wrong button and then he realized his mistake, said, 'Oh, shit', and went into hiding."

"Yeah, he changed his phone number, his email, everything," Tony said. "Well, it don't matter 'cause he don't work here no more, anyways. Not after he done that to somebody."

"I don't think I can sue, and I don't really want to waste time on that horseshit," Jake said. "My name's not on there anywhere and he can always claim it's not me, that it's some other dude, so why bother?"

"Listen to me," Tony said. "That's what you need to do, too, should anybody bring it up, which they probably won't."

"I bet he feels awful," Jake said. "I know he had feelings for me. He wouldn't have done this maliciously."

"You're being generous about it, I'll say that," Tony told him. "*Gallant*, I think is the word!"

Jake groaned, putting his head on the bar. "I just want it to go away."

"Know what?" Tony said. "I'm not sure I'd even be able to recognize you from that there video."

"My mother recognized me right away."

"Well," Tony said, with a wicked grin, "after all, she did *diaper* you."

"I meant my *face*!" Jake slapped the bar and laughed. "I think the neighborhood down under has changed a bit since she saw it last!"

"I gotta ask this, okay?" Tony said. "Curiosity is gettin' the best of me here."

"What is it, Tony?" Jake jerked his chin. "Shoot."

"No smear intended on your sainted mother or nothin'," Tony said, "but how in hell did she even come across findin' this thing of you?"

Jake slouched and released a heavy sigh. "It was forwarded to her from a friend, who forwarded it to her from another friend, who forwarded...."

"Okay, gotcha, like that old game of Telephone." Tony shook his head. "The fuckin' Internet is up everybody's ass!"

They enjoyed a good laugh, and then Tony looked Jake straight in the eyes. "Look, so some people out there are gonna think you're gay, and maybe that Ethan is your lover boy. Big fuckin' deal! People forget, okay? The world moves fast today. Sooner or later they're gonna move onto some other bullshit, and all this here will be yesterday's mashed potatoes."

"From your mouth to..." Jake hesitated.

Tony raised an eyebrow. "From my mouth to...where?" he asked. "God's ears?"

"My mother always said that a lot," Jake said. "My Catholic upbringing, I guess. What more can I say?"

"You still practice?" Tony asked.

"Practice what?"

"Your faith."

"Oh, yeah, Tony," Jake chuckled. "I say a Hail Mary every time I snort coke, and while I'm banging Veronica Marino I always make sure I recite the 23rd psalm. Oh, and the Lord's Prayer is an essential part of every drug drop off, you know, just in case."

"Okay, wise guy," Tony said. "I will have you know that I still go. That might surprise you on account of my connections."

"Go where?" Jake asked. "Church?"

"Yeah," Tony said with a bit of shyness. "Wanna make somethin' of it?"

"Nope," Jake shrugged. "Different strokes, man, different folks."

"It wouldn't hurt for you to give it a try, too, kid," Tony advised. "It don't cost nothin', and it's cheaper than a shrink."

Jake looked at Tony, a playful glint in his eye. "Alright, Tony, you got yourself a deal. I'll give church a shot. Who knows, maybe a little divine intervention can help me out of this mess I've made of my life."

"St. Bridget's is two blocks down," Tony said. "While you're there, put in a good word to send me a couple of dancers, okay? It's down now to just you and Leo."

Jake didn't have the heart to break it to Tony that Leo Shaw was looking to get out. "How 'bout a bourbon first?" he suggested.

"One's your limit, okay?," Tony said, setting up the glasses and reaching for the bottle. "Yeah, I can tell already that this here church thing is gonna be a bust with you."

47. Pier Pressure

WHEN Detective Curtis Pismo called him to come down to Pier 27 and identify Ben Mendelsen's dead body, Jake felt the ground open beneath his feet and swallow him whole.

The eight minute Uber ride to the pier was the longest trip of Jake's young life. Everybody knew that Pier 27 was Max Marino's killing fields, his dumping ground, his message board that clearly spelled out in bold, bloody letters, *Don't Let This Happen to You!*

Jake could venture a guess how Ben managed to end up this way, but why did they contact him to make the identification? And wasn't this type of procedure normally conducted in a room at the city morgue, and not at the scene of the crime, or had he seen way too many movies?

The Uber pulled into the parking area near the entrance to the pier, which had been webbed in yellow caution tape that fluttered in the wind, marking the boundary between the ordinary world and the one of nightmares.

Jake struggled with his Visa card, asking the driver if it was a swipe or a tap. The driver told him it was a tap, and as he grabbed his receipt, he saw two police officers approaching the car.

Jake stepped out of the Uber and into a crime scene illuminated by the flashing lights of police cars. The two officers escorted him to where Detective Pismo was standing. He recognized the detective from his visit to The Velvet Joystick after Marco Santangelo's murder. Marco had been found on the same spot, but that investigation had led to nothing and remained unsolved.

"Mr. Whitney, I appreciate your cooperation," the detective said. "We need your confirmation for the record." He gestured toward the end of the pier, and as Jake reluctantly moved closer, he could make out the twisted nude body of a young Caucasian male.

The salty sea breeze carried a pungent scent of decay, and the moon cast an eerie glow on the scene, emphasizing the dark stains that marred the wooden planks leading to the body. Would he even be able to identify what he was being forced to look at? Jake swallowed hard, attempting to steel himself against the grim reality that unfolded before him. Ben's lifeless form was completely contorted, his limbs positioned at odd angles, a stark contrast to the once lively friend Jake had known.

Detective Pismo, his expression a mix of sympathy and professional detachment, scrutinized Jake's reaction. "Do you recognize this as Mr. Benjamin Mendelsen?"

Jake nodded. "Yeah, that's him."

"Are you absolutely certain?" Pismo asked. "The face is severely battered."

"The scar on his knee," Jake said, exhaling a grief-stricken gust of air. "I was with him when it happened."

Pismo observed Jake's eyes following the trail of bloody bare footprints on the worn wood beneath them.

"We *can* determine that your friend was brought here by whoever killed him," Pismo said. "They stripped him first, we assume. Why else would he be barefooted? And these prints definitely match the size and shape of the feet of the victim."

"How awful...it must have...been...for him," Jake said, on the verge of tears.

"Let's step over here," Pismo said, pulling Jake away from the grisly scene. "Would you like some coffee?"

Jake shook his head and shivered. "No, thank you."

"When was the last time you saw Mr. Mendelsen alive, Mr. Whitney?"

Jake's mind flip-flopped as he tried to remember the last time he saw Ben. It had been a few weeks since they had hung out, but he couldn't remember the exact date. "Uh, it's been a little while," he finally replied.

"Can you give me a rough estimate?" Detective Pismo pressed on.

"Maybe a week," Jake told him, feeling uneasy under the detective's piercing gaze.

"Do you know of anyone who would want to harm the victim?" Pismo asked, taking out a notepad and pen.

Jake knew, of course, but he wasn't about to name names, especially since those names could be connected to himself. He shook his head. "No, I can't think of anyone."

Pismo jotted down some notes. "Did the victim have any enemies you might know of?"

Jake shook his head. "None that I'm aware of. He was a pretty low-key guy. Everybody, uh, seemed to like...him."

"Did he ever mention anything to you about being afraid or in danger?" Pismo asked, looking up from his notepad to meet Jake's eyes.

Jake hesitated for a moment, careful not to put himself in danger by revealing too much. "No, he never mentioned anything like that to me."

Pismo raised an eyebrow, but didn't push the issue. "Well, if you think of anything, please let us know."

Detective Pismo scribbled something down in his notebook, and it appeared to Jake that the detective had more on his mind than he let on.

"Is that all?" Jake asked, feeling a queasiness come over him.

"One more thing," Pismo said, flipping through the pages in his notebook. "Did you ever see anyone suspicious that he kept company with? Anyone who might have wanted to harm him?"

Jake furrowed his brow in an attempt to convey innocence. "No, not really."

"What do you mean by '*not really*'?" Pismo asked, his scrutinizing gaze trying to search the recesses of Jake's mind for any inconsistencies or hidden truths.

Jake shifted his weight from one foot to the other, his eyes darting around the crime scene. "I mean, Ben was kind of secretive sometimes, so I'm not sure who he hung out with when I wasn't around. But I can't think of anyone off the top of my head who would want to hurt him."

Pismo nodded, jotting down more notes. "Can you recall any disagreements or tensions between you two?"

A cold chill ran down Jake's spine. "Am I a suspect?"

"We have no leads as yet, Mr. Whitney." The detective noted Jake's unease and softened his tone. "We're trying to piece together what happened here, and anything you can recall, no matter how insignificant it may seem, could help us."

"Of course, of course," Jake nodded.

"Okay, thank you for your time Mr. Whitney. We'll be in touch if we have any more questions. We'll be happy to drive you home."

"Thanks, " Jake said. "I'd appreciate that."

He felt sick and eager to get away from the gruesome scene. As he walked to the police cruiser, his brain on overload, he wondered why he had been questioned like he was a suspect. Was he also in danger himself? And would he ever be free from the haunting image of Ben's naked, crumpled, and lifeless body?

One thing was certain. Ben Mendelsen was finally cured of his addictions, and would

never, ever place a bet again.

· · · ·

48. Hangin'

BEN Mendelsen's brutal demise was the spark Jake Whitney needed to light the fuse of his redemption. He tried going three full days without a snort or a drink, but fear, anxiety, nausea, tremors, and intense cravings all pointed to withdrawal, and he knew he couldn't do it alone.

He went to the dean of admissions and leveled with her, requesting a month to get himself in shape. He didn't want his parents to know, and since he was of age, they didn't need to be informed. The dean appreciated his honesty and arranged for him to take a thirty day leave of absence.

With Veronica's obsession escalating, becoming more intense and demanding, Jake fabricated a story about some family problems that needed his attention, and he would need to be out of town for a while. She didn't take the news well, issuing threats if he didn't return promptly to her, even though she had voiced disappointment in his recent sexual performance due to Jake's waning libido. Veronica wasn't sure if this was a result of too much coke, too much alcohol, or merely his fading sexual interest in her, although her own increased drug use had her passed out during most of their recent sessions, anyway.

As Jake continued to juggle his job and his studies, his academic performance suffered dramatically, too. He could no longer concentrate on his coursework and assignments, and he found it increasingly difficult to focus during classes. The mounting pressure eventually became unbearable, and he came to the decision to quit his job at The Velvet Joystick. Delivering the news to Tony would be no easy task considering the bar's declining fortunes, forcing a cut back to three shows per week. Jake remained the sole attraction since the departure of Leo Shaw, who had taken Jake's suggestion about writing to heart and decided to detour his dream from laughs to literature.

Jake took a deep breath and pushed open the door of The Velvet Joystick bar, lounge, and strip club. Had it been only six months since he walked into this darkened, forbidding space for the first time?

"Well, look who it is!" Tony called out from his regular station behind the bar as he wiped glasses and stocked shelves.

"How's it hangin', Tony?" Jake was trying his best to be casual and unassuming, dreading the boom he was about to lower on Tony.

"Unfortunately," Tony sighed, "all it does these days is *hang*, kid. Jimmy quit, so now I'm the new bartender, along with doin' everything else in this dump. You watch, I'll be strippin' next, God forbid. How 'bout you?"

"Same old, same old." Jake searched his mind for something to fill in the awkward silence. "Are you married, Tony? I don't think the subject ever came up."

"Nope," Tony replied. "I go my way by myself. You know, like the song says?"

Jake had no idea what song Tony was referring to. "Ever *been* married?"

"Nope, nope, and *nope*," he said. "Why all this sudden interest in my private life? You thinkin' of askin' me out?"

Jake laughed. "Don't let that video of me and Ethan give you any ideas, man."

Tony stopped puttering behind the bar and took a breath. "We need to talk, kid."

Jake eased himself onto a barstool and braced himself. "The last time I heard those four words I wound up sleeping alone."

"Enough of the charade. We're shuttin' down the bar," Tony said. "The Velvet Joystick is closin' for good."

Jake felt bad for Tony, but he was grateful he wasn't going to be the one to break his heart. "As of when?" he asked.

"After Saturday night," Tony said.

"That soon?"

"Max Marino don't mess around," he said. "But I don't need to tell you that, do I?"

Jake shook his head. "So my last dance will be Saturday?"

"Your last dance was last night, kid." Tony reached under the bar, pulled out a white envelope, and slid it across to Jake. "Your final paycheck. I put a little extra to make up for the short notice."

Jake tapped his fingers on the envelope. "Thanks, Tony."

"We're goin' out with just drinks and snacks on tap for our regulars," Tony told him. "No show, just a quiet, dignified exit."

Jake looked up at Tony with concern in his eyes. "What are you going to do after this?"

"I been squirrellin' my extra nuts away for years, kid," he said. "I got a little house in Largo, Florida, right on the water. Time I used it, and time I got away from Max Marino while the goin' is good. I don't want to end up feedin' the gulls on Pier 27."

Jake felt those words cut deep. "I wish you luck, Tony," he said, extending his hand. Tony grasped it and squeezed hard.

"You're a good kid, Jake," Tony said. "The best I ever had here."

"That means a lot."

"What are your plans?" Tony asked.

"I'm going to get clean, get a degree, and get my girl back. If she'll take me back."

"That's a swell plan, kid," Tony said. "And don't go takin' your clothes off no more, okay? Unless, of course, it's an emergency, or you get lucky, you hear?"

"Don't worry," Jake said, and he walked away from The Velvet Joystick left with the haunting question of what lay ahead for him now that he faced the daunting task of rebuilding his life.

49. Lonely End

VERONICA Marino stared down from the terrace of her forty-fifth floor penthouse apartment thinking the people teeming in the street below looked like the ants in the plastic toy farm she played with as a kid. She felt scorn for their pathetic pay-check-to-pay-check existence of never tasting anything fresh, exciting, or exotic. "Humdrum," she muttered to herself. "God save me from humdrum."

Humdrum is what Veronica feared most, aside from aging, of course, and if Jake didn't return, and she was certain he would not, a humdrum life without the young, firm flesh of her twenty-one year old boy-toy would be death itself. She was getting older, and the recent attempts to lure a Jake-successor into her lair were met with polite condescension, like Boy Scouts helping a senior citizen across the street.

In the loneliness of that apartment, surrounded by the useless bric-a-brac of the extravagant life she lived, Veronica found herself in the depths of despair. The drugs that had once promised an escape from the emptiness of her existence had now turned against her, becoming a destructive force she could no longer control. Her descent had reached its tragic conclusion. She was done with it all, and sat alone, waiting for Max to come home to a house filled with the haunting silence of isolation. And she was done with Max, too. He didn't love her anymore, if he ever did, and she was tired of the pity in his eyes when he confronted her escalating use of drugs and alcohol. How else did he expect an aging trophy wife to numb the pain and fill the void of her restless days?

She planned the evening with care. The gun Max had given her as a wedding gift had never been fired. The Sig Sauer P3659 9mm pistol sat nestled in her bedside drawer buried beneath her Adderall, Percodan, Vicodin, Nembutal, Seconal, Xanax, Ambien, Sonata, Lunesta, Avinza, and the treasured Magic Wand rechargeable vibrator.

But on this particular night the gun rested in the pocket of her silk La Perla robe, the same one she bought especially to greet her lover Jake on their steam filled nights.

Veronica pondered the option of waiting a bit when Max walked in, perhaps savoring the moment with some idle chit-chat and a cocktail or three. After all, there was no immediate reason to rush things. But no, no, she had waited long enough and wanted this night over with. She was getting *wet* just thinking about it, as she poured two fingers of bourbon to steady her nerves, and, hopefully, her aim. When she heard the familiar rattle of Max's keys in the door, her heart raced and she felt breathless.

She knew this was it. The moment she had been waiting for. The moment she would finally take control of her life and all the pain and emptiness that came with it. Max's footsteps echoed through the empty hallway, each one a step closer to her freedom. Her hand trembled as she pulled out the gun from her pocket, feeling its weight and cold metal against her skin.

Max entered the room and stopped dead in his tracks, his eyes widening at the sight of Veronica holding the gun. "What the hell are you doin' with that?" he asked, his voice booming.

"I thought of killing myself," she said. "But you're the problem, Max, not me. There's nothing wrong with me that killing you won't cure."

"Are you out of your fuckin' mind you crazy bitch?" he snarled, his face so contorted and ugly she wondered how she had put up with it so long.

Veronica smiled. "What does it look like I'm doing, Max?" she replied, her voice surprisingly calm. "I'm ending it all. The pain, the emptiness, the *humdrum*. It's all going to be over soon."

Max took a step back, fear etched on his face. "You know how much I love you, baby."

"No, I don't know that," she muttered. "You love me? Why do you love me?"

"I love you for a million reasons," he said.

Veronica's tears were flowing. "I'd be satisfied with just one."

Max stretched out his arms in a mock embrace. "You are everything to me, baby."

"I'm nothing, Max!" she snapped. "I'm not even a real blonde. My hair is fake, my nails are fake, my tits are fake, and my marriage is fake."

Max lowered his voice to a whisper hoping to appear less threatening. "Baby, you are as real to me as the sun that shines in the sky."

"Poetry doesn't become you, Max," she said between sobs. "I'm a lonely woman who can't even get it up anymore."

Max looked puzzled. "What do you have that needs gettin' up?"

"Shaddap!" she shouted. "You're always correcting me!"

Veronica's hand was trembling, and she could sense a droplet of sweat running down the side of her face. She imagined the wheels creaking in Max's brain as he studied the odds, weighed his chances, and calculated the distance between them so he could make a grab for the gun. If he succeeded, she knew he would use it on her in a New York minute.

Max reached out toward her. "Come on," he said. "Come to your senses."

"I've come to my senses," she said with a sly smirk. "I'm taking control now, big shot mob boss. I've had enough of this lonely life. I want passion, I want love, and you can't give me either one."

Max's face paled, and he held up his hands in surrender. "Okay, okay, what do you want me to do to make things right?"

"I want you to fucking die," she gasped.

The first shot hit Max in the shoulder, and caused the padding in his suit to puff up and blossom like a flower. He stared at it in amazement, and then turned to face her for a brief moment before lunging. With his face only a few inches from hers, she took aim and blew his nose right off his face. The proboscis flew to the left, while his cumbersome body fell to the right in slow motion, shaking the entire room, maybe the entire building, as it crashed to the floor like a giant felled oak tree. She chuckled to herself wondering if a mob boss falls and there's no one in the room to hear it, does it make a noise?

Veronica called out his name, and then jabbed him in the side with the toe of her Gucci mule. She stared down at his lifeless form for what felt like hours, but was actually no more than a few seconds. "Yup, he's deader than Nixon's dick," she muttered to herself.

She took a deep breath and glided over to the gilt-framed full-length mirror in the atrium hallway to check her reflection and ensure that her makeup was still flawless, her blonde hair cascading perfectly over her shoulders in loose waves, and her blue contacts sparkling in the bright glare of the Carrara marble walls surrounding her. She had always been told that she was beautiful, and her favorite expression was, *"So I'll die young and leave behind a beautiful corpse."*

Okay, so she wasn't what anybody would call young anymore, but the thought of getting even older made her blood run cold. So when she jammed the barrel of the Sig pistol into her vagina and pulled the trigger, that took care of that.

50. Starting Here, Starting Now

THIRTY days. Thirty. *Long.* Days.

Jake Whitney stood in the doorway of the rehabilitation center as the sun dipped below the horizon, casting long shadows across the quiet city streets. The building behind him had been the crossroads of his life, a place he went to when he could no longer deny the need for change, and he hoped the dangerous path he had been on was behind him as well.

He recalled the day he arrived, his heart pounding in his chest, staring at this same ominous entrance as if it were the gates of hell. That first day now felt like a dream to him, but someone else's dream.

It all started with what is called an intake interview, where a staff member asked him questions regarding his substance use and his lifestyle—information used to customize his treatment plan. He then met his counselor, Frank, a friendly and comforting guy who put him at ease and explained the structured life he could expect at the center.

His day started at 7 AM, followed by breakfast, meditation, physical wellness training, relapse prevention training, reflection time, nutritional training, recovery meetings—activities conducted entirely in a communal setting to ensure that he would never be alone. There were breaks for lunch and dinner, of course, with each day ending promptly at 10 PM. Grinding his behind under the hot lights at The Velvet Joystick would be a cakewalk compared to his new basic training routine.

The night before his release, he didn't sleep a wink. Except for his exit interview with Frank, he had no idea what he was going to do with the brand new day that had never been touched.

Jake sat on the other side of the desk as Frank greeted him. "So how are you feeling?"

"Not sure," he shrugged. "Scared, I guess."

Frank nodded. "It's normal to feel scared after spending so much time in such an intense situation. I'm proud of you, though, and I'm proud you chose this road to recovery. Your progress has been tremendous."

"I couldn't have done it without your support," Jake said. "Or without your pep talks."

"Of course, you would have," Frank said with confidence. "You wanted it badly enough. That's what got you through it."

Jake took a deep breath. "I'm so afraid I might fall back into my old habits."

Frank shook his head, "No, you won't. But that fear is a good thing. It will keep you fighting, ready to challenge any temptation. Fear is a great motivator, Jake."

"Tell me about it," he said with a chuckle.

"What's next for Mr. Jake Whitney?" Frank asked.

Jake rubbed his hands together in expectation. "Well, I start classes tomorrow morning, and the next day I go back to serving overpriced half-caff mocha lattes to pampered have-it-alls."

Frank tossed his head back in laughter, but he held his finger up as a warning. "Put the cynicism aside, young man," he said, "and don't be so judgmental. Remember, there was a time in the not-so-distant past when you were hooked on some pretty expensive stuff yourself. And I don't believe what you craved was readily available in coffee shops."

"You're right, Frank." Jake threw up his hands. "Shame on me."

"No more feelings of shame," Frank said. "Promise me?"

"I promise," Jake said.

As Jake walked out of the rehabilitation center, he felt the warmth of the sun on his face and took a deep breath of fresh air. It was time to start over, to rebuild his life, and to make amends for his past mistakes. He pulled out his phone and scrolled through his contacts until he found the name he was looking for. He hit the call button and waited for the person on the other end to answer.

After three long rings, the machine picked up. "You've reached the voicemail of Sarah Miller. Please leave a message at the tone."

"Who says '*tone*'?" he muttered to himself. "Everyone else says, 'Please leave a message at the *beep*.'" Then he heard the tone...or beep...and he panicked for a second before collecting his thoughts. "Yeah, hey, this is, uh, this is Jake, and, uh, well..."

"If you're calling me, sir, I'm not home at the moment," said the soft, clear voice. But it wasn't coming from the phone.

Jake turned and wondered how she had managed to sneak up without him hearing a thing. "Sarah," he said, in a soft, nearly inaudible, whisper.

She looked at him with tear-filled eyes. "Didn't you used to strip at The Velvet Joystick?"

"Oh, I am so, so very sorry," he said, as a mile-wide smile beamed across his face. "You must have me confused with somebody else."

····

THE AUTHORS

Grace Sidney Harold lives in the Midwestern United States and loves steamy novels so much they decided to write a few themself, including *Wednesdays are for Strangers, Mister Erogenous,* and *Rhonda on Top.*

Kevin Barry Collopy was born in New York City, and is the author of the play *In Rebel Country,* which was produced Off-Broadway, as well as the plays, *Distracted by the Landscape, Track & Field,* and others, which have been performed in New York, Los Angeles, and the United Kingdom. His previous novels are, *I Shouldn't Have Been That Sentimental, Toxurbia, Shopping Hungry, Short Time Dead,* and *The Swoon Hypothesis.*

All reviews are appreciated! Good, bad, or indifferent, let us know about your reading experience.

Thank you!

Milton Keynes UK
Ingram Content Group UK Ltd.
UKHW010658090524
442467UK00001B/23